The Herring Seller's Apprentice

L. C. TYLER

The Herring Seller's Apprentice

❖

A GRIPPING TALE OF MURDER, DECEIT AND CHOCOLATE

MACMILLAN NEW WRITING

For Ann, Tom and Catrin

First published 2007 by Macmillan New Writing
an imprint of Pan Macmillan Ltd
Pan Macmillan, 20 New Wharf Road, London N1 9RR
Basingstoke and Oxford
Associated companies throughout the world
www.panmacmillan.com

ISBN 978-0-230-52965-0

1 3 5 7 9 8 6 4 2

A CIP catalogue record for this book is available
from the British Library.

Typeset by Intype Libra Ltd
Printed and bound in Great Britain by
MPG Books Ltd, Bodmin, Cornwall

Disclaimer
It is, in real life, possible to buy chocolate (and many other useful things)
from Karen at the Findon Newsagency, and Peckham's Celebration Sausages
can be purchased from Tony at the butcher's. Catrin has occasionally
been known to walk Thistle on Nepcote Green.
All of the other characters in this book are fictional.

Mais il faut choisir: vivre ou raconter.

– J. P. Sartre

Postscript

You'll have found the same thing yourself, of course. Just when you think you have committed the perfect crime, things most unfairly take a turn for the worse.

The phone had rung in an ominous tone, breaking the small-hours silence for me and most of West Sussex. I had picked up the receiver quickly and listened for a few moments to a familiar voice trying to do irony at one o'clock in the morning – something that is as difficult as it is pointless. This was, however, only a clumsy precursor to the real purpose of the call. 'You've finally slipped up. I know exactly what your game is, you pillock.'

'I doubt that,' I said. I was quite calm. I may possibly have yawned. But I was definitely calm.

'I know who you're off to meet.'

'Do you?' I asked. 'I bet you don't.'

'You bet I do. The only thing I don't quite understand is how you've got away with as much as you have.'

'Unmerited good fortune,' I replied. 'And the fact that I'm

a writer of detective stories. That, I suspect, played a large part in it.'

There was a snort of derision from the far end of the phone line, a snort as yet unjustified, because, the more I thought about it, the more certain I was that I could turn this to my advantage.

And however many evasions and half-truths there had been over the preceding months – those long months between my return from France and this unnecessary midnight phone call – I had just spoken one unquestionable truth. I *was* a writer.

Of that at least there could be no doubt.

One

I have always been a writer.

I wrote my first novel at the age of six. It was seven and a half pages long and concerned a penguin, who happened to have the same name as me, and a lady hedgehog, who happened to have the same name as my schoolteacher. After overcoming some minor difficulties and misunderstandings they became firm friends and lived happily ever after; but their relationship was, understandably, entirely platonic. At the age I was then, hedgehog-meets-penguin struck me as a plot with greater possibilities than boy-meets-girl.

Little has changed. Today I am three writers and none of us seems to be able to write about sex.

Perhaps for that reason, none of us is especially successful. Together, we just about make a living, but we do not appear on the best-seller lists in the *Sunday Times*. We do not give readings at Hay-on-Wye. The British Council does not ask us to undertake tours of sub-Saharan Africa or to be writer in residence at Odense University. We do not win the Costa Prize for anything.

I am not sure that I like any of me but, of the three choices available, I have always been most comfortable being Peter Fielding. Peter Fielding writes crime novels featuring the redoubtable Sergeant Fairfax of the Buckfordshire Police. Fairfax is in late middle age and much embittered by his lack of promotion and by my inability to write him sex of any kind. When I first invented him, sixteen years ago, he was fifty-eight and about to be prematurely retired. He is now fifty-eight and a half and has solved twelve almost imposs-ible cases in the intervening six months. He is probably quite justified in believing that he has been unfairly passed over.

Under the pen-name of J. R. Elliot I also write historical crime novels. I am not sure of J. R. Elliot's gender, but increasingly I think that I may be female. The books are all set in the reign of Richard II because I can no longer be both-ered to research any other period. It is a well-established fact that nobody had sex between 1377 and 1399.

As Amanda Collins I produce an easily readable 150 pages of romantic fiction every eight months or so, to a set style and a set formula provided by the publisher. Miss Collins is popular with ladies of limited imagination and little experience of the real world. A short study of the genre had already revealed to me that doctors were the heroes of much romantic fiction – usually they were GPs or heart surgeons. I decided to choose the relatively obscure specialty of oral and maxillofacial surgery for mine. Oral and maxillofacial surgeons have a great deal of sex, occasionally with their own

4

wives. But they do so very discreetly. My ladies prefer it that way, and so do I.

The three of us share an agent: Ms Elsie Thirkettle. She is the only person I have ever met, under the age of seventy, named Elsie. I once asked her, in view of the unfashionableness of her first name, and the fact that she clearly has no great love of it, why she didn't use her second name.

She looked at me as if I were an idiot boy that she had been tricked into babysitting by unkind neighbours. 'Do I look like a sodding Yvette?'

'But why did your parents call you Elsie, Elsie?'

'They never did like me. Tossers, the pair of them.'

My parents did not like me either. They called me Ethelred. My father's assurance that I was named after King Ethelred I (866–871) and not Ethelred the Unready (978–1016) was little consolation to a seven-year-old whose friends all called him 'Ethel'. I experimented with introducing myself as 'Red' for a while, but for some reason it never did catch on amongst my acquaintances. Oh, and my second name is Hengist, in case you were about to ask. Ethelred Hengist Tressider. It has never surprised anyone that I might prefer to be known as Amanda Collins.

It is possible that all agents despise authors, in the same way that school bursars despise headmasters, head waiters despise diners, chefs despise head waiters and shop assistants despise shoppers. Few agents despise authors quite so openly as Elsie, however.

'Authors? Couldn't fart without an agent to remind them where their arses are.'

I rarely try to contradict remarks of this sort. Based on

Elsie's other clients, this is fair comment. Many of them probably could not fart even given this thoughtful assistance.

Elsie does in fact represent quite a number of other authors as well as the three of me. Occasionally we ask each other why we have settled for this loud, plump, eccentrically dressed little woman, who claims to enjoy neither the company of writers nor literature of any kind. Has she deliberately gathered together a group of particularly weak-willed individuals who lack the spirit either to answer her back or to leave her? Or do we all secretly enjoy having our work and our characters abused? Neither answer is convincing. The real reason is painful but quite clear: none of us is terribly good and Elsie is very successful at selling our manuscripts. She is also very honest in her criticism of our work.

'It's crap.'

'Would you like to be more specific?'

'It's dog's crap.'

'I see.' I fingered the manuscript on the table between us. Just the first draft of the first few chapters, but I had rather hoped that it would be universally hailed as a masterpiece.

'Leave the literary crime novel to Barbara sodding Vine. You can't do it. She can. Or, to put it another way, she can, you can't. Is that specific enough for you or would you like me to embroider it for you on a tea cosy in cross stitch?'

'I've put a lot of work into this manuscript already.'

'Not so that you'd notice, you haven't,' said Elsie kindly.

'But I've just spent three weeks in France researching the damned thing.'

'It won't be wasted. Send Fairfax to France. He deserves a break, poor bugger. Is France the place for him, though?

He doesn't seem to have any interests beyond police work, Norman fonts and local history.'

'He's a crack addict, a drag artiste and he played for Germany in the '66 World Cup. My gentle readers suspect nothing as yet, but it's all in the next book.'

'It had better not be. Your gentle readers take that loser Fairfax very seriously and do not appreciate irony in any form. Sergeant Fairfax is your bread and butter, and twelve-and-a-half per cent of your bread and butter is my bread and butter. If Fairfax starts hankering after fishnet tights, send him round to me and I'll sort him out.'

This also was true. Elsie would sort him out. I once tried to give Fairfax an interest in Berlioz (I must have been reading too much Colin Dexter). Elsie had the blue pencil through that before you could say 'Morse'. 'Don't bother to develop his character,' she said. 'Your readers aren't interested in character. Your readers aren't interested in atmosphere. Your readers aren't interested in clever literary allusions. As for allegory, they won't know whether to fry it in butter or rub it on their piles. They just want to guess who did it before they get to the last page. And don't give them more than ten suspects, or they'll have to take their shoes off to count them.'

Perhaps I should have said that if there's one thing that Elsie despises more than her authors, it is anyone foolish enough to buy our work. But again, I would hesitate to contradict her.

To tell the truth, I rarely try to contradict Elsie on anything these days. That was why, sitting in my flat that evening, all those months ago, I knew that the first draft would remain for ever just that. But it was worth one more try.

'You could take the manuscript back to London with you,' I suggested, 'and read it properly.'

'The problem,' she said tartly, 'does not lie with my reading, and my waste-paper bin in London is already quite full enough, thank you. Do you know how many crap first novels there are out there?'

'No,' I said meekly, not having counted them.

'Too many,' said Elsie, not having counted either, but with a great deal more confidence in her opinions. 'Now, how was France?'

I sighed. 'Totally redundant from a literary point of view, apparently, but otherwise very pleasant. I stayed in a charming little hotel. I sat by the Loire and drank the local wine – Chinon mainly, but sometimes Bourgueil. I absorbed a great deal of extremely authentic atmosphere. The sun shone and the birds sang. I met nobody who had ever read one of my books. Bliss.'

'Useful research.'

I sensed the irony in her voice – not a difficult achievement, since Elsie and subtlety are not even casual acquaintances. 'My characters were going to spend a considerable amount of their time sitting by the Loire drinking wine,' I said. 'I pride myself on accuracy. I had to research it in depth.'

'Bollocks. Did you have sex with anyone?'

'No.'

'I thought the French shagged anything that moved.'

'Not in Châteauneuf-sur-Loire. Possibly all manner of

depravities were practised in Plessis-les-Tours or Amboise, but I never went to either.'

'Well then, next time, try Amboise. Hang loose. Get laid. Write it up in your next book.'

'Not *my* next book. As you well know, I don't do sex. And, though I cannot be absolutely certain in this matter, I don't believe that I have ever hung loose.'

'Is that why your wife left you?'

'My ex-wife,' I said. 'To be pedantically accurate, my ex-wife. Geraldine and I were incompatible in a number of respects.'

'The main way in which you were incompatible is that she was screwing your best mate.'

'Ex-best mate,' I said. 'He is my *ex*-best mate.'

'Then the cow walked out on you.'

'You make it sound rather abrupt and uncaring. She stayed long enough to write me a very touching note.'

'All right, she's a literate cow,' Elsie conceded generously. She's a fair woman in some ways, though not many. 'Is she still with the chinless wonder?'

'Rupert? No, she left him a while ago.'

She narrowed her eyes. 'You seem better informed than you should be, Tressider. Don't tell me you're still in touch with the old slag?'

'I must have just heard it from somebody. Why should you think I'm still in contact with her?'

'Because you're a prat, that's why. I'd like to think that you were too sensible to go within a hundred miles of her. Normal people in your position – not that I know many normal people in my line of work, of course – sever all ties with their ex. Making a wax effigy and sticking pins in it is also said to be good. I could get you some wax if you like. There's this Nigerian bloke down the market. He does pins too.'

'I think that it's quite possible to be friends with a former spouse,' I said. 'Geraldine and I must have had something in common, after all. We had a number of happy years together, though admittedly she was simultaneously having a number of happy years with somebody else. Life's too short to be bitter over these things.'

'OK, Ethelred, stop just there, before I sick up. You've just never learned to hate properly, that's your problem. Stop being nice and start wishing she was rotting in hell. Clearly I'm not saying that you should have to do it single-handed. Geraldine had a very special and remarkable talent for making enemies, and there'll be lots of others wishing hard along with you for her early and preferably messy demise. But frankly, if she ever turns up murdered, just remember that it is your absolute right to be considered the prime suspect.'

'But that's hardly likely to happen,' I pointed out.

The doorbell rang.

It was a policeman.

He smiled apologetically.

'I have some bad news, sir,' he said. 'It's about your wife. May I come in?'

Two

I rather like policemen.

I am not one of those authors who write of bumbling incompetent flatfeet who have to be aided by keen-eyed amateur sleuths. Why should I? The amateur detective never existed. I do not know of a single genuine case (and I have now studied many) in which an elderly spinster living in St Mary Mead has afforded the police the slightest assistance. Real cases are not solved by flashes of genius, but by large numbers of people gathering and sifting even larger quantities of information. Criminals are caught by house-to-house inquiries and by tedious hours of studying security-camera pictures frame by frame. Or you get lucky and a close and esteemed colleague grasses them up. The police, in my experience anyway, rarely take the trouble to gather all the suspects together in the drawing room of a country house to announce the result.

But there is a long and particularly English literary tradition of gentleman (and lady) sleuths from Sherlock Holmes, through Lord Peter Wimsey and Miss Marple, to Brother Cadfael. I would hesitate to knock anything that makes money for honest and deserving writers, but it's a load of twaddle, frankly. In my novels, as in real life, the police investigate murders; the public do their bit by getting murdered. Though one may criticize the Sergeant Fairfax novels for many things, perpetuating the myth of the amateur detective is most certainly not amongst their faults.

It was not, however, a fictional Sergeant Fairfax from Buckford standing at my door. It was a flesh-and-blood constable from the West Sussex Police.

'You'd better come in,' I said.

The delicate question of whether Elsie should remain for this possibly awkward interview was quickly solved.

'You two just carry on. Don't mind me,' she told us both; and she settled back in her chair, arms folded, daring us to evict her. I looked at the policeman; he looked at me. We noted each other for the cowards that we clearly were and proceeded to make the best of a bad job.

He gave an officious cough, half in Elsie's direction, and said, 'I am afraid that I have to tell you that your wife is missing.'

'My ex-wife. We were divorced some years ago.'

'Your ex-wife, of course. For the moment she has simply been reported as a missing person. My apologies for putting this so bluntly, but we have good reason to believe that she may have committed suicide.'

I remained, though I say it myself, admirably composed.

'I am very sorry to hear that,' I said, 'but I can't see what it has to do with me. Not after all this time.'

'When did you last see your wife, sir?'

'My ex-wife?'

'Your ex-wife.'

'I can't remember precisely.'

'Have you seen her in the past fortnight?'

'I've spent the past three weeks in France, officer. I got back yesterday evening.'

He noted this in a small book that he was carrying.

'Châteauneuf-sur-Loire,' I said. 'Would you like me to spell that?'

He raised his notebook slightly so that I would not be able to see what he had written. 'I don't think that will be necessary,' he said, with a nicely judged degree of contempt for the general public that Fairfax would certainly have commended. 'Do you know of any reason why she might have wanted to commit suicide?'

'I can't pretend to know for certain, but she might have had several good reasons. She has perpetual money problems: her first business went bust round about the time we split up. She went into a second venture with her sister. I think I heard that that was in trouble too. She has also just finished a relationship – quite a long-standing one.'

'And her former partner was . . . ?'

'Rupert Mackinnon. She must have been with him about ten years. I'm not sure of his current address.'

He noted these details without comment.

'I am sorry,' I concluded, 'but I don't think that I can help you much more than that.' I stood up, preparatory to showing him out. He remained seated.

'We had hoped that you might be able to tell us a little

13

more, sir. You see, Mrs Tressider left what we assume was a suicide note in her car before she vanished.'

I nodded. 'And?'

'She left the car quite close to here – by the beach at West Wittering.'

I sat down again. 'Bloody hell,' I said.

'Quite. That's a long way to come from North London to commit suicide. I mean, it may be a coincidence, your living in West Sussex and her leaving the suicide note in West Sussex. But you will see why it struck us as odd, sir, if you know what I mean.'

It struck me as many things, though 'odd' was perhaps not the first word to spring to mind.

'So, she never lived down here, did she, sir?' he continued, as if to clarify for me an interesting fact concerning my domestic arrangements. He narrowed his eyes, leaving an ominous accusation hanging in the air that I did not like one bit.

'No, I moved here after we split up.'

'Then there's the suicide note.'

He showed me a photocopy of a sheet of what had clearly been headed writing paper. The very top of the sheet had been roughly torn off, leaving a jagged edge, but a few letters of the address could be made out, including 'N1'. There was something before and something after, but you couldn't tell what, unless you knew the address that had been there. Which I did, of course.

'Your wife lived in the N1 postal district of London?' He raised an officious eyebrow.

'Yes. Barnsbury Street, Islington.'

14

'So it looks like her paper. But what we can't work out is why she tore the top off like that. The wording's funny, too.'

I took the note with growing trepidation and read it. It was written in lively block capitals, with playful little curls on a random selection of letters. It read as follows:

TO WHOMSOEVER IT MAY CONCERN. DEAR SIR OR MADAM, I HAVE HAD ENOUGH. BY THE TIME YOU READ THIS I WILL HAVE GONE TO A BETTER PLACE. FAREWELL, CRUEL WORLD ETC. CORDIALLY YOURS, G. TRESSIDER (MRS)

'I mean,' said the constable, 'nobody writes "FAREWELL, CRUEL WORLD" on a suicide note, do they? Not in real life. You don't even get that in detective stories, for goodness' sake.' He gave a contemptuous sniff.

I've seen (and written) worse clichés in crime fiction myself, but perhaps he read nothing but P. D. James and had higher standards than I did. 'Sorry, officer,' I said. 'Having had only a few seconds to look at it, I really am not in a position to speculate on the wording. You say it was left in her car?'

'That is correct: a red Fiat.'

I must have shown surprise because he quickly added, 'It was a hire car, not her own. She'd collected it from Hertz at Gatwick airport a few days before it was found. She'd rented it for a week – paid for with her credit card. She must have driven it down to West Wittering the same day, left the note in it and then . . .' He paused. 'Well, of course, we don't know what happened then. As you will be aware, you have to pay to take your car to the beach there. The gates at West Wittering beach are locked at eight thirty at this time of year. The guard noticed the Fiat on Tuesday when he was doing his final rounds. There are often a few cars still parked there, left by people who've gone for a walk along the coast and forgotten the time. There's a charge for being let out after the gates have closed, but most are usually gone well before midnight. This car was still there the following evening when the guard did his rounds. It was a nice new one too – just 300 miles on the clock – not some dumped old banger, like you get all the time now round here. So he took a closer look and saw this note on the seat. Nothing else in the car, by the way – just the suicide note and the Hertz paperwork. That's when we were called in. We discovered that your wife had not been home to Islington for a day or so, but her neighbours remembered that you had moved down here, quite close to the Witterings.'

'I am deeply grateful,' I said, 'to her neighbours for pointing this out. Nevertheless, I would remind you that West Wittering is forty-five minutes' drive at least, even if you don't get held up going round Arundel.'

'Bloody Arundel bypass,' he said with a nod. Then he sucked on a tooth for a bit before adding, 'You don't know where she might have left her own car, do you, sir?'

'No. Absolutely not. What sort of car does she have now anyway?'

'It's a Saab convertible. Metallic black with alloy wheels. Nice cars, them Saabs. Good cornering. Decent bit of acceleration. That's missing too, you see. But it may show up. It could even be in for repairs somewhere, hence the hire car.'

He asked me a few more questions, feeling no doubt that he owed it to the Council Tax payers of West Sussex to cover the matter comprehensively; but there was little that I could usefully tell him, other than to repeat that it had been a while since I had been in touch with Geraldine and that, much though I wished I could help, I had no idea where Geraldine was or why she should have abandoned a perfectly good hire car on a Sussex beach.

'So,' said Elsie, when I had shut the door behind him, 'what would Fairfax make of that, eh? A woman vanishes close to the residence of her ex-husband. She leaves a cryptic suicide note in block capitals – not in her usual handwriting – and in a car apparently hired for the purpose.'

'Last Tuesday the ex-husband was busy not having sex in Châteauneuf-sur-Loire, a long way from the place where she vanished.'

'But why would anyone hire a car to commit suicide in?' asked Elsie, with her agent's eye on the bottom line. 'Why not use your own car? It's cheaper.'

'You heard what he said: perhaps her own car was in for a service or something.'

'Why get your car serviced if you're about to kill your-self?'

It was an obvious thing to ask, and I wished I had Gerald-ine there to provide an answer. I had almost thought of a reply when Elsie decided to answer her own question.

'I have three theories,' said Elsie, prematurely ticking off the hypotheses one by one on her podgy fingers. 'First theory, right? She did top herself, and did it in Sussex to cause you as much grief as possible. But that doesn't explain the missing-car issue, thus I am obviously not too keen on that one. So (therefore), second theory: she did not top herself at all but is very much alive and is sitting in a pub somewhere laughing at us.'

'Why should she do that?'

'I don't know, do I? Maybe she's faked a suicide and done a runner to avoid her creditors. Or maybe she's done it all for a giggle.'

'All right then: she's killed herself or she hasn't. That's still only two theories,' I said.

'I haven't finished,' said Elsie, with a dismissive wave of her fat little hand. 'I'm the detective for the moment. At best, you're just a suspect.'

'Sorry,' said the suspect.

'Theory number three: perhaps somebody's murdered her and made it look like suicide.'

'That's possible,' I said with a slight but carefully judged shrug.

'No, it isn't – it's just wishful thinking,' said Elsie, sighing deeply. 'All these little twists and turns are Geraldine to a T. Take that missing car, alloy wheels too: the whole business of switching cars would seem totally unnecessary to anyone except Geraldine. So would that note: "I've gone to a better place." You bet she has. She's done a runner. I won't believe she's dead until I see the body – and possibly not even then.'

'There may never be a body,' I said, pulling the discussion back to the suicide theory. 'The currents off that beach are pretty strong. She could have been swept right out into the Channel.'

'Only if she could be arsed to go into the water,' said Elsie, staring out of the window at the buildings opposite in the fading light. 'And at the moment, there's nothing to suggest that's what she did. I'd lay a pretty large bet that she is still out there somewhere, warm and dry, spending somebody else's money.' She seemed to be casting her glance at Peckham's the butchers, just opposite my flat; but there was no sign of Geraldine wildly buying chops and Peckham's Celebration Sausages with her ill-gotten gains – only Tony could be seen inside the shop, moving briskly, meticulously sweeping and washing everything down before closing.

It was a peaceful scene: a Sussex village at dusk, with the summer moving gently towards autumn. Flint-walled houses with warm mossy roofs, one more pub than was strictly necessary, a post office and an Indian take-away, all cradled within the smooth and now darkening slopes of the South Downs. For most of the inhabitants, another uneventful day was about to be followed by another peaceful night. The Worthing-bound traffic on the bypass was no more than a distant murmur. A number of birds had, quite properly, decided that it was time for their evening chorus. Everything was just as it should be. This was, after all, a place where retired people came from London to grow old and die quietly in their beds, not a place for bizarre suicides in low-mileage red Fiats.

'Look,' I said, 'let's leave this to the police, shall we? It is fortunately their job to find my wife, dead or alive. I agree that Geraldine would be perfectly capable of faking a suicide purely for the fun of the thing. But I shall leave my wife to the police.'

'Your ex-wife,' said Elsie.

'My ex-wife,' I said.

Three

In the beginning writing was pure pleasure. It was Elsie who taught me that, with only a little effort, it could just as easily be mindless drudgery.

It was Elsie too who taught me that the royalties on a 300-page book are generally greater than those on a 200-page book, even if the story could be told better in 200 pages. ('Add fifty per cent more suspects,' she advised.) It was Elsie who insisted on a new Fairfax book every year, with a publication date to coincide with the purchase of Christmas presents. (She had a theory that people bought my books to give to others rather than to read themselves.) It was Elsie who helpfully suggested that plots could be endlessly recycled because my readers had the attention span of a gnat with Alzheimer's. (For once I ignored her.)

My first Fairfax book, *All on a Summer's Day*, was written when I was very young indeed – not yet twenty-five – and while I was still working for the Inland Revenue as the most junior of trainee tax inspectors. Writing was then – how can

I express this? – a shiny box, brimming with an inexhaustible supply of chocolate of every possible type, whose textures and flavours I could still only guess at. I relished every word, trying for some perfection that I knew must be possible and, I think, almost achieved in that first novel. The plot must have come to me in a single flash, because I don't remember having to alter it significantly as the book progressed.

Fairfax, drinking heavily and barely tolerated by his colleagues, is on the verge of early retirement. A murder inquiry is being closed without an arrest or any real progress. Fairfax, as the least useful member of the team, has been left to tidy up the paperwork while others move on to more promising cases. There is no pressure to finish the task quickly – indeed, Fairfax's colleagues are praying that it will keep him out of their way until his farewell party. In a strange way, it suits Fairfax too – never a team player at the best of times and increasingly comfortable with his solitary drinking bouts and lonely task. In his more sober moments, however, Fairfax works his way methodically, the stub of a cigarette dangling from one corner of his mouth, through the evidence that has been collected.

My story opens on 6 July – the anniversary of the date of the crime, and a stiflingly hot day. Fairfax's brain has not been called upon to work at full stretch for some time, but there is something about the case that has troubled him almost since the start: a feeling that they have overlooked the obvious. While glancing at his till receipt during a refreshing liquid lunch at the White Hart, it suddenly strikes Fairfax that 6/7 on a receipt might mean 6 July or 7 June, depending on whether you write the day or month first. This is perhaps more obvious now than it was then, when only Americans wrote dates backwards. He leaves his third pint almost untouched and returns to his desk. Sure enough, one key assumption ultimately rests on a single small piece of evidence – a receipt – that gives the date not as 6 July but as 6/7. With trembling nicotine-stained fingers, Fairfax goes back through the statements again, this time discounting this piece of evidence. It is like a crossword puzzle in which an early answer has been incorrectly entered, making a nonsense of later clues.

Now that this small false step has been corrected, other seemingly unimportant fragments slip into place. Sitting at his desk, Fairfax reruns the whole inquiry, using the evidence that they had all along, but from this new starting point. By the end of the afternoon he has solved in a day what the team failed to achieve in a year. I concluded the story not with the arrest of the suspect nor even with the chief constable congratulating Fairfax, but with Fairfax happily surrounded by disorganized heaps of paper, waiting for the inspector to come in and ask him whether everything has been filed yet.

The book ran to less than 150 pages and, because the action takes place in a single day, has a particularly satisfying structure. Apart from the brief visit to the pub and back, the action does not shift from the room in the police station. I enjoyed playing with recurring metaphors such as an unfinished crossword puzzle on Fairfax's desk, and dropping early clues about the ambiguous nature of dates through the medium of Fairfax's own historical studies. It was the only Fairfax book that I can say I really enjoyed writing and it is perhaps ironic that it is the only one that is now out of print, being (in the view of my publisher) incompatible with the later fast-moving plots and scrupulous attention to the detail of modern police investigations. By the time I wrote the second Fairfax book I had Elsie as my agent and was taking a harder and more commercial approach to literature. Today I look at that box of chocolates and it seems to be empty except for a couple of unwanted coffee creams that are all that now remains of the very bottom layer.

I think that Fairfax both sensed and resented the change in my attitude and he became, if anything, more introverted and secretive. He stepped back, it has to be admitted, from open alcoholic excess, but I could tell that he was still drinking quite heavily on the quiet. Most writers will tell you of the strange phenomenon by which the characters they create take on a life of their own. Fairfax, like Elsie, often seemed to disregard my opinions completely.

It was in the second book, *A Most Civilized Murder*, that I decided to give Fairfax an interest in church architecture. I knew before I did so that he would have strong views, but I had no idea how quirky they would prove to be. I quickly found that he had no time for Perpendicular, the very glory and summit of English high Gothic, referring to it disparagingly as 'spiky'. He also despised Decorated and Early English. The only true church architecture for Fairfax was solid, gloomy, cavernous Norman. Even Transitional, with its tentative move away from the semicircle and towards the pointed arch, he viewed as effete, decadent and suspect. As for Wren, that dickhead had completely lost the plot: St Paul's was a mere pagan temple, unworthy of the name of a Christian church.

Having discovered Fairfax's preferences, I immediately gave Buckford a pristine and unaltered Norman cathedral, which he thereafter visited frequently, though with no especial show of gratitude. When, at a much later stage, I started to have to draw maps of Buckford, I realized that in *All on a Summer's Day* Fairfax must have walked past the cathedral twice without a glance or a single comment. But, as I have said, the book is now out of print, and nobody is ever likely to spot that strange anomaly.

How Fairfax manages to reconcile his idiosyncratic but nevertheless very genuine Christian piety with his secret drinking bouts and unfathomable pessimism is something that he keeps locked deep inside his policeman's soul, and has never revealed to me.

I had scarcely shown Elsie out of the flat, when the bell rang yet again.

I must explain that Findon, where I now live, though large for a Sussex village, is en route to nowhere except Worthing. Friends from London did not habitually drop in on their way to and from other places. Elsie occasionally forsook her office, as she had that afternoon, to visit me rather than vice versa, but more usually I made the journey up to Hampstead to see her. Friends from Findon, such as I had, rarely called unannounced. Days, often weeks, passed without anyone ringing the bell of my small flat in Greypoint House. My immediate reaction was therefore that Elsie had left something behind or that the police had returned with additional questions. Nothing had quite prepared me for who it would be.

'Rupert?' I asked, because I was for a moment genuinely uncertain.

Middle age is cruel to the truly beautiful. I am neither more nor less remarkable now than I was when I was twenty. But for the *jeunesse dorée*, middle age can prove a dramatic fall from grace.

I had known Rupert well during his own golden-youth epoch. We had read the same subject at the same college. We were not inseparable – indeed I now realize that, in a strange way, we were scarcely even friends. But he chose, for reasons of his own, to spend a great deal of time in my company.

He was tall, blond, aristocratic and improbably good-looking. I was tall. There was no situation, no society, no geographical location in which Rupert looked anything other than at home and at ease. I rarely felt at home anywhere – least of all when I actually was at home. Perhaps he felt my ordinariness acted as a counterpoint to his own charm and beauty. If so, it would never have occurred to him not to use this fact to his advantage, nor would it have occurred to him that he needed to offer anything in return. I remember one occasion, when we were together in a restaurant, I had thanked the waiter for some small service – possibly fetching me a clean knife or filling my glass with water. 'You don't need to thank him all the time in that disgustingly servile manner,' said Rupert. 'It's his job, Ethelred. It's what he's *for*.' Amusing Rupert, providing him with alcohol, making him look or feel better – these were simply the things that I was for.

The first time I met Rupert could, I suppose, have been at the principal's sherry party for freshers at the beginning of

Michaelmas term; but large gatherings at which he was not the centre of attention were not conditions under which Rupert considered that he could be appreciated at his best. I do not remember his being at the party and quite possibly, contrary to all custom and precedent, he chose not to go. What I do recall very clearly is a day or two later, when he arrived unbidden at my rooms at college and, with only the briefest of introductions, draped himself instinctively in the only chair without broken springs and announced, 'Somebody usually gives me a drink round about now. I don't mind what it is, as long as it's the best. If you don't know what's the best, just give me the most expensive.' I had been trying to write an essay, did not want company and had little enough money to buy my own alcohol, let alone other people's. That evening Rupert got through half a bottle of malt whisky before leaving unsteadily, but just as abruptly as he had arrived. I later found that he had been sick on the staircase as he departed, something for which my scout blamed (and never quite forgave) my immediate neighbour.

'Somebody usually gives me a drink round about now.' It was a very Rupert phrase. So was, 'It's been such a pleasure to see me.' Some people – the majority of people, I think – found Rupert intensely irritating, but others could not resist succumbing to his peculiar charm. I couldn't. Later, in a much more comprehensive manner, nor could my wife.

There was a theory, amongst the girls in our year, that Rupert was homosexual. When I pointed out that he had innumerable girlfriends, they merely gave each other knowing glances and said, 'Exactly.' I had no girlfriends, but nobody felt the need to attribute this to my sexuality.

Geraldine first entered my life as one of Rupert's transitory companions. She was two or three years younger than we were and was, at the time, at one of the secretarial colleges that flourished as a sort of distant penumbra of the university. In some ways she was Rupert's perfect counterpart – a lively blonde with almost perfect legs, a seductive smile and eyes that sparkled with a constant mischief. She anticipated by some years the fashion for dressing in black that, much later, everyone seemed to adopt. I am not suggesting that she was in any way fashion-conscious, still less a leader of fashion. Indeed, she usually dressed very simply in a sweater or polo-neck and a skirt just short enough to display her black-stockinged legs to the best possible advantage. But black suited her and she knew that it suited her.

I met her from time to time, in Rupert's room or punting on the Cherwell or at parties; then she was replaced, with no warning at all, by Victoria or Amanda or Kate or somebody. After university, Rupert and I worked in different parts of London. Victoria or Amanda or Kate was replaced by Elizabeth, a pleasant, sensible, but wholly unremarkable girl who was training to be a nurse and who seemed unlikely to hold Rupert's interest for long. If I thought of Geraldine at all it was only in the context of a tenner that she had borrowed from me and clearly never intended to return. In due course, Rupert married the sensible Elizabeth. I was only mildly hurt at not being asked to be best man.

It was some time after that that Geraldine reappeared, not to repay my tenner, either immediately or at any stage in the future, but to invite me to a dinner party. She made some polite chit-chat about my last book (I was a proper writer by then – not just a biographer of penguins) before, apparently as an afterthought, asking whether I could let her have Rupert and What's-her-name's new address. At dinner (there were about a dozen of us squeezed into her small flat) Rupert was seated next to Geraldine. Elizabeth and I were at the far end of the room; Geraldine scarcely exchanged more than a dozen words with either of us all evening. But she then surprised me by phoning up the following day and suggesting a trip down to Kent – with Rupert and What's-her-name if they could be persuaded to come. Could I speak to Rupert? I spoke to Rupert, who immediately said that he rather thought they were free that weekend. His enthusiastic response struck me as odd at the time, though not of course with hindsight.

If I said that Geraldine married me to get closer to Rupert it is unlikely you would believe me, but later I was never able to come up with any better reason. The only really solid argument against this theory is that Geraldine never thought far enough ahead for that type of long-term planning. Of course, it is possible that she saw in me something that I was never able to see in myself – at least for a while. But, if so, I still have no idea what that thing could have been and sometimes wish that she had told me. The knowledge might have helped me in the bleak years that followed.

Elizabeth later told me that she had been onto Geraldine's game from the very beginning, though, that being the case, it is difficult to see why she then allowed Geraldine to steal her husband quite as easily as she did. As for me, I was not onto Geraldine's game until the day she walked out, leaving me a brief note propped against the salt cellar on the kitchen table.

'Do you mind if I come in?' asked Rupert. He made a nervous attempt at the old Rupert smile. 'I should have phoned you first, I suppose, but I wasn't sure that you would agree to see me. It's rather important, you see.'

Once inside, Rupert stood uncertainly in the middle of the room, nervously rubbing his hands together, the half-smile now rigid and fixed. He seemed somehow smaller than when we had last met. The once-perfect skin was perfect no more; there were lines round the mouth and the eyes. The fair hair was just a bit too long and was noticeably thinning. His manner, once languid and urbane, now seemed merely vague. I could see, for the first time, why Elsie might choose to describe him as 'chinless'. Above all, he looked old and tired.

'I suppose I couldn't ask you for a drink, dear boy?'

'I take it somebody usually gives you a drink round about now?'

For the first time he grinned properly, acknowledging this throwback to our earlier days.

'Whisky?' I suggested.

'Perhaps a small one if it's not too much trouble. Do you mind if I sit here?' He paused awkwardly, waiting for me to confirm that my hospitality extended to seating.

I offered him the most comfortable chair and fetched him a large malt whisky. I could at least (just) afford it these days, and I no longer had any reason to bear him ill will. Even at the time of the divorce I suppose that it was Elizabeth, and for some reason Elsie, who had taken such exception to his role in the break-up of two marriages. Now, some ten years on and deserted by Geraldine in his turn, Rupert was not somebody that I could hate, much though this weakness might lower me in Elsie's estimation.

'This is very awkward,' he began. 'Very awkward indeed.' He toyed with the heavy cut-glass tumbler, a piece of flotsam (as it happened) that I had rescued from the wreck of my marriage. He swilled the whisky first one way and then, in an experimental fashion, the other. It seemed there were only two ways to swill whisky, so he was forced to come to the point. 'You know that Geraldine has done a runner?'

I didn't want to talk about this to Rupert, but I realized that, for all sorts of reasons, I had no choice. If I had had the foresight to pour myself a drink I also could have done the swilling thing, but I just said, 'That's what Elsie thinks. The police on the other hand seem to think it's suicide. Money problems possibly.'

'But that's not like Geraldine, is it?' he said with a nervous quickness that would have been quite untypical of the old Rupert. He frowned as though he was trying to make sense of it all. 'People like Geraldine go around screwing everyone else up. It's like water off a duck's back to them. Even if she had money problems, that wouldn't have made her kill herself.'

'Anything, anything at all, could be like Geraldine. You never could tell what she would do next.'

Rupert nodded, but with a far-away look in his eyes. 'Do you know what I thought – when I first heard that she had vanished and left that odd note? I thought – Elizabeth has bumped her off and faked a suicide to cover up. She was always threatening to murder Geraldine in the old days.'

'Surely not?'

'Oh no, I don't think so now.' Rupert ran his fingers quickly through his hair. 'It's a long time since she sent Geraldine a really specific death threat. I mean, place, time, order in which bits were to be cut off with a chain-saw. In any case, she'd have less cause to do anything now – with me and Geraldine no longer together. You know we split up, I suppose?'

'Yes.'

He nodded again. Unlike Elsie, he did not seem curious about how I knew.

'But then,' he continued, 'Elizabeth remarried and moved to Essex or somewhere dreadful like that. Why *does* anyone live in Essex? She's got kids now. Elizabeth wouldn't have done it. But it isn't suicide either. That means Geraldine is alive somewhere. We have to find her, Ethelred.'

'We?'

Rupert tossed back the last of his whisky. 'OK, point taken. Not your problem any more. It shouldn't be mine now that we're no longer . . . well, you know . . . but there was some unfinished business that meant we had to stay in touch, like it or not.'

He looked at me and then suddenly changed tack: 'Look, I'm sorry about this. It was wrong of me to come. I could understand if you still hated my guts, old boy.'

I said nothing, but replenished his glass.

'I would if I were in your shoes – hate me, I mean,' Rupert blundered on. 'I went off with your wife, you know.'

So, there it was: yet another unnecessary reminder about my private life. Though my memory is becoming worse in middle age it was unlikely, on the face of it, that I would have forgotten my best friend going off with my wife.

'You went off with the only woman I ever loved, if you don't count my primary schoolteacher,' I said. 'She may possibly be the only woman who ever loved me. Apart from my mother, I suppose, though she was sometimes rather vague on that score.'

'Only woman who ever loved you? That's worse,' said Rupert. He shook his head slowly.

I knew Rupert and I knew whisky. In spite of long years of training, he did not have the strongest of constitutions for alcohol. The first glass was making contact with his bloodstream. Soon he would be feeling very sorry for himself. Another couple of glasses and he could be crying on my shoulder. If I let him stay that long and gave him that much whisky. But I planned to do neither.

'It's much worse,' he said again, as if it was important that he should persuade me of the justice of his earlier remark. He jabbed a finger in my direction to emphasize a point that really required no emphasis at all. 'I'm a shit. If I were you, I'd be sitting there thinking "bastard".' He brushed back a thin but wayward lock of blond hair that had flopped into his eyes.

I was in fact thinking 'poor bastard', but I did not say so. I was also wondering whether he could afford a haircut these days. But I didn't say that either. 'Since you're not me,' I observed, 'you can't tell what I should be feeling. Unlike Elizabeth, I never sent any death threats, did I?'

'Very decent of you, old man. Very white, if you don't mind me saying so.'

Very white. I often wondered where Rupert found some of his phrases. Many were facetious affectations that he had picked up in his teens or twenties and seemed to have been unable to drop. But, even in that distant past that constitutes my teens, nobody our age said 'very white of you' or 'old boy' – except just possibly in the patrician circles from which Rupert seemed to come.

'But perhaps not *white* enough to spend time looking for Geraldine,' I observed, with only slightly too much emphasis on the word 'white'. I could afford just a little mockery and he would have no choice but to put up with it.

'Let me at least tell you why I've got to find her,' said Rupert, staring at a spot on the carpet about five feet in front of him.

'Go on.'

'You know how Geraldine was always coming up with hare-brained schemes,' he said. 'Well, just before we split up she devised one of her very best. She'd got wind of plans for a new tube line in the East End. She was going to buy property in Hackney, do it up and sell it on when the new tube line was announced and prices rose.'

'And they didn't?'

'No, they're going up, I suppose – everything in bloody London is and everybody's making money out of it except me. It's just that there never was much evidence of any property buying on Geraldine's part. Once or twice I pointed out that she had the money and we were about to miss the boat, not to mention the expenses she was running up, but she said that she still needed to raise more dosh.'

'Very inconvenient for her.'

'Not for her. You know Geraldine. It was my money that she was playing with. Probably other people's too. I think her sister invested as well.'

'How much?'

'I don't know about other people, but it was two hundred thousand of mine. Every penny that I had, and then some. Strangely, when we split up, my first reaction wasn't to demand my money back – in fact, I was afraid she might cut me out of the deal. The doubts started later.'

'But she can't have made much of a loss if she didn't buy anything. You must be able to get most of it back.'

'Only if I can find Geraldine. If she's done a runner, she's done it with my cash.'

Two hundred thousand pounds would have been a great deal of money to me, but then I'm just a poor writer. I tried to recall what Rupert now did. I seemed to remember that he was a fund-raising consultant, which might bring in a great deal or nothing at all. Looking at him, I suspected that nothing at all was closest to the mark and that the loss of that sort of money (could he have inherited it?) mattered very much indeed. And he was relying on me, it seemed. Under the circumstances, things did not look too good for Rupert.

'I don't think I can help,' I said abruptly. 'I really have no idea where she is.'

'Shit. I was sure, for some reason, that you would.'

'Why?'

'It was just . . .' He paused and gave me what I can only describe as a funny look. 'I just thought you might *know*. You see . . .' There was another pause as though he had been about to confide something to me but had suddenly changed his mind. 'Sorry, it was just a silly idea I had.'

'Very silly,' I concurred.

The last remaining fragment of Rupert's backbone seemed to collapse. His head sagged forward and for a moment I thought that he was about to burst into tears. But he merely gave a deep sigh and straightened himself up again.

'The problem is,' he said, 'you can never say "no" to her. She gets into your system, and once she's there you can never quite shake her off – a bit like malaria. Look, you've even still got her photograph over there on that table.'

We both turned and looked at the slightly faded snap of a still-young Geraldine with her blue eyes, short blonde hair and a smile of the purest wickedness. When had I taken that? On the trip to Kent, when I still scarcely knew her, but was already in the process of losing her?

'I would have thought that a crime writer like you would have been dying to investigate a problem like this,' said Rupert, who clearly shared at least one of Elsie's delusions.

'No,' I said. 'It is a popular misconception that crime writers have the first idea how to solve a real case. Most police sergeants can't write best-sellers either. This is one of the many times when things are best left to the professionals. I am a writer and that is all I am.'

'Geraldine reckoned that you only lived for your writing. She had a nickname for you.'

'I know,' I said. 'The Herring Seller. It was a facetious reference to the red herrings that she considered my stock in trade. I never found the name quite as amusing as she evidently did.'

'She never did consider other people's feelings that much,' said Rupert wistfully.

From her photo frame Geraldine grinned at us out of the past, daring us to wonder what was going on in her mind.

It must have been around ten o'clock when Rupert finally accepted that I was going to do nothing for him and left, which in turn would mean that it was about quarter past ten when the telephone rang.

'Is that double-dealing bitch with you?'

It might have been more charitable to at least ask who the caller was referring to, but I just said, 'No, Geraldine isn't here.'

'Well, when she does show up, just say that all this clothes-on-the-beach business doesn't fool me for a moment. I want my money back, and I want it now.'

'I see . . .' I began, but the caller had already hung up, leaving me to try to identify her voice. Of course, Charlotte, Geraldine's sister and erstwhile business partner. She had clearly fared no better than Rupert. I could only speculate how much she had been persuaded to part with. Charlotte was nobody's fool, but she would resent the deception that much more in consequence.

The probability that Geraldine was alive and had successfully left the neighbourhood with a considerable amount of other people's money was becoming so strong that the next call came as something of a change of pace.

'Good evening, sir. It's Detective Inspector Cooke here. I'm sorry to phone you so late, but we've found a body. We think that you may be able to identify it for us.'

Four

Perhaps at no time other than our own could a man reach comfortable middle age without confronting a dead body in the cold flesh.

I had of course seen my share of corpses: Vietnam, Cambodia, Rwanda, South Africa, Bosnia had nightly provided a procession of bodies, mutilated and unmutilated according to the taste of the winning side, on my television screen. But not a real live dead corpse. Everything now conspires to separate the living and the dead.

When my father died, I was away at university. We Tressiders were not the sort of family to leave bodies carelessly strewn around the house. By the time I returned home my father was safely boxed up and ready for disposal in the normal, seemly manner.

When my mother died some years later, happy and prematurely senile in a hospital in Poole, there was some delay in contacting me and I arrived to find that she had been removed to the mortuary. A plump, unctuous young man

38

with a smooth pink face asked me whether I wished to see my mother's body. I must have paused for a moment, because he quickly added, 'Many people prefer not to. It can be distressing. Very distressing.' His gaze was directed at the floor rather than at me, but since the floor seemed unlikely to feel distressed, I replied on its behalf.

'Most people prefer not to?'

'Not under the circumstances.'

I wondered what he meant. Then I remembered that my mother had, years before, agreed to donate various parts of her body for transplantation or research, as the doctors in their wisdom saw fit. Perhaps he meant that very little that was recognizable remained. Would it be in bad taste to ask which bits they had taken? Heart? Lungs? Kidneys? Eyes? Assorted offal?

'Whatever you think best,' I said awkwardly.

'I think you are very wise,' he said, softly congratulating the floor.

Later it occurred to me, rather uncharitably, that at my mother's advanced age she would have had little that even the most desperate transplantee would have coveted. Perhaps it was nothing more than that the modern etiquette is simply not to view a dead body. Or the young man may have just been reluctant to take me on the long walk down to the mortuary at the end of a hard day. But that equally uncharitable thought came much later.

'There are some papers that we need you to sign,' he said.

I took a much shorter walk to an untidy office and signed them, thus missing my second chance to view a corpse.

Now, in middle age, I had been offered another appointment with death, and this time I was not sure that I wanted it. There was, however, little possibility of escape. I was led inexorably along a corridor and into a room full of white tiles and gleaming stainless steel. In the middle of the room was a table and on the table was a shrouded form, with a provisional claim to being my late ex-wife.

Perhaps it was the lifelong build-up to this moment, but the instant when the sheet was finally pulled back to reveal a head and shoulders was strangely one of relief.

The face that I saw, in a way so familiar but in a way so unfamiliar, was that of a woman in early middle age with short blonde hair. What mischief there had been in the smile in life had been replaced by a singular serenity. Sergeant Fairfax, looking over my shoulder, drew my attention to the fact that the hair had been recently dyed – the colouring was unnaturally even, but there was no trace of dark roots showing. The hair also seemed to have been cut only a few days before. Make-up had been carefully applied – eye shadow, bright red lipstick. The red jacket, the top of which was showing above the stiff green sheet, looked new in spite of some muddy stains. If this was suicide, then she had wanted to be a smart corpse.

'We immediately assumed that it was your wife,' said the young policeman who had accompanied me there. 'But we do need you to confirm the identification.'

'I see,' I said.

'So, you are able to identify the body, sir?'

Just for a moment – but only for a moment – I was tempted to say, 'Officer, I have never seen this woman before in my life,' if only to see the look of consternation that I knew it would cause. But I am not the sort of person who plays cheap tricks. That was always Geraldine's forte.

'I understand that it's been some time . . .' he began, apparently as much to fill in time as anything. In this place there seemed to be a great deal of time to fill.

'I would know my wife anywhere, officer,' I said quickly and firmly.

'You've no doubt about that?'

'None at all.'

The young constable breathed a sigh of relief. 'We are very grateful to you for identifying the body, sir. I realize that you and she have been divorced for some time. We might have asked her sister, but she does live some way away and it would have been . . .'

'Very distressing for her?'

'Exactly, sir. Very distressing.'

'That was thoughtful of you. Where was the body found?'

'Up on Cissbury Ring.'

'Cissbury?'

'That's quite close to you, isn't it, sir?'

'Fifteen minutes' walk – maybe twenty.'

He looked at me a little oddly. I saw his point. The action was getting closer and closer to home.

'She was found late this afternoon. A man walking his dog,' the policeman added. Now that he had a firm identification, the real work of the evening seemed to be over and he was becoming quite chatty. 'She was hidden amongst gorse bushes in one of the old flint pits. *Strangled*.' He laid particular emphasis upon this last word.

Fairfax tutted that I had not spotted the slight bruising round the throat.

'Strangled,' I repeated. 'And . . .'

'No, just strangled really. Your wife's body was found fully clothed – quite expensively clothed, to the extent that I am able to judge, Italian anyway. But no handbag, purse, wallet, driving licence, jewellery. Just the one shoe so far – high-heeled, also Italian, also red. In view of the missing items, for the moment we have to assume robbery was the motive.'

Or perhaps somebody wanted to remove the things that would identify her, I thought.

'The murderer took everything then?' I asked.

'We did find one thing nearby, though it's not clear whether it belonged to your wife,' said the policeman. 'A rather soggy paperback called *Professional Misconduct* – a romantic novel by—'

'Amanda Collins,' I said.

'Well, fancy your knowing that,' he said, much impressed.

'You will find that its hero, Mr Colin Cream, is eventually exonerated by the GDC and marries the loyal and faithful dental nurse. I only know because I wrote it. Amanda Collins is just a pen-name.' I smiled modestly.

This however did not impress him. My actually being Amanda Collins clearly devalued, in his eyes, my earlier achievement of knowing who wrote *Professional Misconduct*. Fortunately I have long since learned to manage without praise and admiration.

'Your wife enjoyed romantic fiction, did she, sir?'

'Enjoyed? No,' I said. 'Not as far as I know.'

We both turned again to look at the body – a few moments ago a nameless thing found by a dog, now Geraldine Tressider. A real person again with a unique identity, a bank account, a national insurance number, an ex-husband. (She currently had no credit cards, passport or driving licence, but she probably wouldn't be needing them.) I wanted to stroke the forehead, to smooth away the pain as one does, I would imagine, with a sick child. But of course, I didn't do any such thing. We Tressiders don't.

'How long had she been there?' I asked.

'We still have to wait for the pathologist's report, but we think just a couple of nights – which fits with when her car was left at West Wittering.'

Or to put it another way, when I was in France. 'Excellent,' I said.

'Excellent?'

'I mean, I assume that is all for the moment?'

'Just one or two more questions, sir,' said the policeman. 'But not here.' He nodded in the direction of the body. I doubted that she would either hear or interrupt, but he was still calling me 'sir' and I reckoned that the questions would not be too difficult to handle. Accordingly I allowed myself to be led out of the gleaming room and back along the corridor to the world of the living.

'A man walking his dog' – the phrase kept recurring to me in the taxi back to Greypoint House. It always brings a very clear picture to my mind. The man is dressed in a tweed jacket, cavalry twill trousers and heavy brown brogues. He has a small, carefully trimmed moustache and quite possibly a peaked cap. The dog is quite large – an English setter or a pointer. It capers around, tail wagging, ears flopping stupidly, then dives into some bushes. Suddenly there is frantic barking. The man frowns and calls the dog. 'Jess! Come here!' There is no response. 'Jess, come!'

He turns and starts to stride purposefully towards the bushes, little suspecting what is to follow.

To be quite honest, I too, at that point, had little idea of what would happen next.

Five

My father spent his life perfecting failure.

I imagine that, in his youth, his ambition must have been a chair in Anglo-Saxon at Oxford or Cambridge. By the time I was old enough to be aware of him as a possessor of ambitions, he had considerably lowered his sights to a lecturership at one of the new universities that were then springing up. He faced the problem however that, even for one of these quite plentiful appointments, he would require published work. But, at the same time, no reputable journal was likely to publish his papers unless he had a university post or some other evidence of academic credibility. While he was trying to see a way round this little difficulty, he taught English at a local state secondary school.

There he blighted many A-level prospects by insisting that all of his pupils received a thorough grounding in *Beowulf* before he was prepared to introduce them to other texts that merely happened to be part of the curriculum. It is perhaps surprising how long the school was willing to tolerate this eccentricity. It took four or five years before he was relegated to teaching the lower forms, where it was felt he could not inflict any significant damage on young minds. Nevertheless, several generations of bemused first and second formers still had to endure *Widsith*, *Deor*, *The Ruin*, *The Wanderer* and *The Battle of Maldon* as their introduction to secondary school English.

I can still see him quite clearly (because for one excruciating term I was in a class that he taught), his tall frame perched precariously on the edge of his desk, his glasses balanced equally precariously on the end of his nose, his book held stiffly in front of him, declaiming verse.

I dwelt with Franks, with Frisians and among Frumptings
the Rugians I knew, and the Gloms and Rome-Welsh.

It was from these particular lines that my father eventually acquired the nickname 'Glom', which, all things considered, was one of the most positive developments to come from his poetry readings. The name rather suited him and, had the boys really disliked him, they were capable of coming up with nicknames that were very much worse than that.

Sometimes, in desperation, he would try one or two of the Saxon riddles, hoping that their clumsy double entendres would appeal to our adolescent sense of humour.

'"*Swings near his thigh a miraculous object! It hangs below the belt, midst the folds of his garments, stiff and hard, with a hole in its front.*" Well, what do you think that can be, Thompson? Eh?'

His mild blue eyes would scan the class, desperately pleading with each of us to share the joke. But while the class would often laugh uncontrollably during tragic epics or love poems, my father's attempts at humour would invariably stun them into horrified and embarrassed silence.

Being in his class for English was, however, infinitely preferable to being taken by my father for games. The news that their football match was to be refereed by him was always greeted by the teams concerned with loud groans and pitying looks in my direction. My father's attitude to football was simply this: that it was a singularly unimportant activity and that it therefore mattered little whether he followed the strict rules of the sport in question. I believe that he did in fact have a better grasp of the laws of the game than any of us (he certainly had a number of books on the subject at home) but he seemed to delight in awarding free kicks or disallowing penalties in the most cavalier and arbitrary manner. His refusal to see that, for us at least, each game mattered enormously, was the closest my father ever came to deliberate cruelty. But time spent on a muddy sports field was, for him, time utterly wasted and he would have scorned to pretend otherwise.

He used to say to me that if he could only teach just one child to love the beauty of Anglo-Saxon poetry, then his life would not have been entirely in vain. It is doubtful however whether even this relatively modest ambition was achieved. When I went to university I elected to read geography, even though I preferred both history and English, on the grounds that geography was a subject wholly untainted by any contact with Angles, Saxons, Jutes or Gloms.

But by that time my father had discovered that whisky could be an excellent substitute for ambition, or indeed life. I don't believe that he ever registered either my treachery or even the fact that I had left home.

Later, after I became known for my detective novels, people would ask me whether I had based the pessimistic and introspective Inspector Fairfax on anyone I knew. I have always replied 'no'. Though my father had good cause to take a dim view of life, he remained in fact an incurable optimist, right up to the day that he committed suicide.

'You'd have thought that a decent pub would have at least stocked Cadbury's.' Elsie deposited onto the wet table a pint of beer for me and a lemonade for herself. Alcohol was not her vice. Chocolate was.

I placed my glass on a beer mat, the one small dry island on an oak table well watered by its previous occupants. Elsie plonked her glass unconcerned in the beer lake that lapped around it. She was dressed that lunch-time in a sort of turban and long flowing garment that I would have had difficulty in giving a precise name to, though I did not doubt that it was the height of fashion. Elsie was a small plump woman who insisted on dressing like a tall willowy one. It was a strange vanity for somebody who was, on the whole, entirely free of vanities of any sort.

'So they gave you a grilling, did they?' she asked, rescuing the dampening sleeve of her robe from its place on the table. 'Did they fingerprint you? Don't try to spare your feelings: just tell me every humiliating detail.'

'Fingerprints, yes, as a routine precaution. But not a

grilling, Elsie, far from it. It is clear that I am not in any sense a suspect. In addition to identifying the body, they merely wished me to confirm where I had been over the past four days.'

'And . . .?'

'You know perfectly well. I was in France until the day before the body was found.'

'So let's get this straight,' said Elsie. 'We are being asked to believe that your wife—'

'Ex-wife.'

'—drove to West Wittering, either to fake a suicide or genuinely kill herself. She then walked away from the car, done up to the nines, and just happened to run into the Cissbury Strangler on her way out of the car park. Or bleeding what?'

'The balance of probabilities,' I said, 'would seem to favour "or bleeding what".'

Visitors to West Wittering wore shorts and T-shirts in the summer, Barbours and Hunter wellies in the winter. As long as it was not actually snowing, they carried cool boxes and buckets and spades. Preferably they had dogs. Even when inspecting the body, it had struck me how incongruous it would have been for Geraldine or anyone else to have left the car park at West Wittering beach dressed in a red jacket and skirt and red high-heeled shoes. She could not have failed to be noticed as she walked back down the long, straight and open approach road into the village. She would have been an utterly dog-less, red, Italian beacon in a world of English greens and browns. And nobody had as yet come forward, it seemed, to report a sighting.

'So,' said Elsie, 'was she killed somewhere else and her car left at West Wittering with a note written by the killer?'

'Possible,' I said.

'But the note was on her own paper. Which means that the murderer must have known her well enough at least to get hold of it.'

'Perhaps the paper was already in the car,' I suggested.

'What for?'

'How should I know? A shopping list, perhaps.'

'It had the top torn off,' mused Elsie.

'That need not be significant,' I said. 'It was just a bit of scrap paper that happened to be available. I know a red herring when I see one. Trust me. I'm a hack writer.'

Elsie considered this point and nodded several times more than I felt was strictly necessary. 'All right then, what about this? She was planning to run off with somebody else. He picked her up from the car park – or even left the car and the note there with her knowledge. Then he double-crossed her. Lured her up to Cissbury Ring and strangled her.'

'Why should he, when he could have drowned her at West Wittering much more convincingly?' I asked, half facetiously. But Elsie seemed to take this objection equally seriously.

'Maybe they fell out later over the division of the loot? Maybe he discovered that she was going to double-cross him?'

I could well believe that double-crossing on this scale had always been a regular part of the home life of my dear ex- (now officially late) wife. But I just said, 'Don't you think that this is getting a little far-fetched?'

'Why do you keep raising all of these objections?' Elsie demanded. Nobody did narrowed eyes quite like her.

'Because this is not a problem for us to solve. The police are already working on it. They have road blocks out there at this moment, questioning people going up to Cissbury Ring. They are going through databases of known criminals. They're out fingerprinting the sheep for all I know. How can we compete with that, sitting in a pub with no chocolate?'

'What would Fairfax say if he heard you now?'

'He'd say quite right too. Fairfax has no time for amateur sleuths or for any policeman with less than thirty years' experience.'

'But just think if we solved this ahead of the Old Bill. Think what a book it would make.'

'Who is this "we" of whom you so glibly speak? Don't jump from the first person singular to the first person plural without checking there are at least two people with a desire to do some amateur sleuthing. From where I'm sitting, I can count only one – unless you are planning to join forces with Rupert. He also mentioned the word "we" in a similar connection, as I recall.'

'Oh, come on . . . Ethelred . . . Red . . . Reddy Baby . . . I could be your apprentice. Please.'

Hard-nosed and foul of tongue though Elsie might be under most circumstances, there was a distinct little-girly side to her – at least when it stood a better chance of success than other means.

'Elsie, no.'

'What if I said "pretty please"?'

'I would not recommend it as a course of action likely to be successful.'

'Oh, all right. But let's just take a stroll up to Cissbury Ring, shall we? I could do with some exercise. Drink up, Tressider. You're going walkies.'

So, there it was. When pleading failed, she could always revert to ordering me around.

The route from the Gun Inn to Cissbury Ring lies first along a road lined with low, bricky suburban bungalows, then skirts Nepcote Green's willows and pretty flint cottages before climbing gradually but unrelentingly towards the broad skies and sheep-nibbled turf of the downs. When the road stops at the National Trust car park, the real scramble up to the iron-age fort begins.

Elsie, whose training for events of this sort consisted of an evening in front of the television with a large box of Thornton's Continental Selection, puffed a little as we climbed the last few steps and stood on the grassy rampart. The wind flapped against her unsuitable but undoubtedly fashionable robe. None of this however, for the moment, seemed to disconcert her.

Sussex was rolled out before us, in every possible shade of green and brown, sweeping from one misty horizon to the other. Cloud shadows drifted over the rounded chalk escarpments and dipped capriciously in and out of dry valleys. In this vastness of earth and sky the works of man seemed insignificant pinpricks. Here and there the slopes were dotted with tiny white sheep. In a field below, what appeared to be a toy tractor chugged backwards and forwards, harrowing or drilling or gleaning or whatever one does in a tractor in the autumn. The idea that it might have been a child's toy was accentuated by its bright primary colours – blue, red, yellow – in a landscape of leaf and earth. The thought of Geraldine on her (alleged) long walk away from West Wittering car park again flashed briefly in front of me.

The September air had as yet no trace of winter's hardness and the smell of the warm damp soil wafted up to us from the newly ploughed fields. Summer was still giving way reluctantly to autumn. The harvest was in. Soon leaves would start to dry, redden and fall. It was a scene to inspire anyone with poetic thoughts.

'Well, one thing's sodding well certain,' said Elsie. 'Your missus was done in up here. Nobody would drag a body up a slope like that.'

'There might have been a gang of them,' I reminded her mischievously. 'The robber band dividing the loot amongst themselves by moonlight.'

'Bloody hell, Tressider. Do get a grip,' said Elsie. 'Now, let's see if we can find out where the body was discovered.'

This too seemed unlikely, but on the flat ground in the centre of the ring we found small pieces of blue-and-white plastic tape hanging from a bush, indicating that the police had recently cordoned the area off. It was in one of the many rough, bramble-filled depressions that pockmark the site – old flint workings that pre-date even the construction of the earth ramparts. Originally they would have been thirty foot deep or more, but now they offer at best only a temporary hiding place for an unwanted corpse.

'Not where *I* would choose to hide a body if I wanted it to stay hidden,' said Elsie, echoing my own thoughts. 'But good enough for a day or two while you put a few miles between yourself and the West Sussex Police.'

'So you don't think that it was planned?'

'Spur-of-the-moment job, in my opinion.' She puffed out her chest as she said it. She was getting into being a herring seller's apprentice.

'Meaning?'

'There can be no doubt that your wife was planning to do a runner with other people's cash. Before she could make her getaway somebody stopped her, killed her, took the bunce – and all of her ID – and left the body here. The business of the car at West Wittering is a red herring that somebody has planted to throw us off the scent. Mark my words.'

'I see,' I smiled. 'So, you think that in real life criminals have the leisure to plant red herrings?'

'All right, I'm no more certain than you are; but don't try to adopt that bloody superior tone with me, Ethelred Tressider, until you're selling over ten thousand copies in hardback. Until then I'm as entitled to my views as you are. Now, let's list the suspects.' She deposited her round little body on a bench, and pointedly ignored the splendid view that lay in front of her and below her. 'There's Rupert, obviously, the dumped boyfriend. There's Elizabeth, dumped wife of the afore-mentioned chinless loser, equally obviously. You say that Charlotte was also not exactly on good terms with her sister, so we add her to the list. Then there's Mr X.'

'Who's that?'

'Whoever she was planning to do a runner with. There must have been somebody.'

'Why?'

'Jesus! Which of us is the sodding crime writer? Because Geraldine never dumped one man before she had moved on to the next. If she got rid of Rupert, it figures that there was somebody else.'

'Not necessarily.'

'Get real, Ethelred . . . please? In case you have forgotten, your ex-wife was a Grade One Listed slut. She was a floozy of architectural and historic importance. This is a simple case of *cherchez le bloke*. Identify Mr X and the case is halfway to being solved.'

'Geraldine isn't . . . wasn't . . . like that,' I said. 'She might sometimes have given the impression . . . but you never really knew her.'

'I knew her well enough. How many men do you think she'd had affairs with before she finally left you for that idiot?'

'Affairs? None at all,' I said. 'It was just Rupert.'

Elsie shook her head sadly, then suddenly stood up and smoothed down the front of her robe with a quick movement of her palms. 'If that's what you want to believe, Ethelred.' For a moment she looked at me almost tenderly – goodness knows why. Then she rubbed her hands together. 'Now, what time does that village post office close? I have an appointment with a half-pound bar of Cadbury's finest hazelnut.'

And we set off, each lost in our own thoughts, down the hill, then onwards to the post office and (for one of us at least) the absolute certainty of chocolate.

Six

My fear is not that I shall one day look back on the last half-dozen years as dreary and utterly wasted. My fear is that one day I shall look back on them as the best days of my life.

But of course, it could be, and has been, much worse. Much worse. When Geraldine walked out on me, one of the many things that friends said to comfort me was that two people as selfish and self-centred as her and Rupert would never be able to stay together for long. This proved, by modern standards at least, to be somewhat wide of the mark. They remained together for just over ten years. But even at the beginning, I could have told my well-meaning comforters that they were wrong.

Though Rupert appeared, on casual inspection, to be utterly tied up in Rupert, his selfishness was of a studied and, ultimately, totally artificial kind – a mere facade. 'Mere' however does not do justice to the facade that Rupert created over the years. It was a facade of such depth, a facade with so much apparent solidarity, that those who knew him only casually frequently mistook it for the real thing.

Once one had penetrated a layer or two of this remarkable edifice, he could be disarmingly honest about its construction. Rupert on one occasion said to me, 'For every affectation I have, I can date precisely, sometimes to the minute, when I acquired it and who I acquired it from. Some of my secondary mannerisms are taken from literature, but I like to work directly from nature if possible. Take the way I write the letter P, for example – that was copied from somebody at prep school, whom I greatly admired at the time. I never liked his Bs, however, which are from another source entirely. Many of my very best mannerisms are from my old Latin master, who had once been in the West African colonial service. It may look pretty easy to be me, but I can assure you that you have to work like a black to do it properly.'

From which real or imaginary person he had copied the air of self-centredness, I never did find out, but it was no more than the first outer layer of the pseudo-Rupert, and most people who knew him penetrated it quite early on. Though Rupert was undeniably quite capable of using people to achieve his ends, he could also show surprising generosity. He would lend people money, his clothes, his car, with quite genuine unconcern for their ultimate return. To lend Geraldine £200,000 – if he had it – would have been an extreme example of this trait, but no more than that. Though it was unclear where Rupert would have laid his hands on that type of money, it never occurred to me, in the days and months that followed, to question even once the veracity of his claim. It was part of the pattern. In his way he genuinely cared about people. After his failure to ask me to be his best man he quickly compensated for this lapse by assuring me that I would be godfather to his and Elizabeth's first child. That they chose not to have children did not lessen, in his eyes or mine, the honour that he was trying to bestow on me.

Geraldine's self-centredness too was not entirely straight-forward. It was the selfishness of a small child who knows what she wants, and it was as easy to forgive as that of a small child. She wanted everything in the shop window. Nobody had ever quite found a way of explaining that this would not be possible.

More often than not she got her way, even when the odds seemed stacked against it. She had, for example, a phobia about dentists, and never visited one, to my knowledge, during her adult life. But her teeth were always immaculate. Whether this was just one of many examples of life's unfair-ness or whether Geraldine simply took great care of her teeth, I cannot truly say – but an unexpected side of her character was her single-minded determination when she really wanted to achieve something. Perhaps that too was child-like in a sense.

She certainly had a child's impulsiveness. There was little that so typified her approach to life as the way that she played chess. A careful build-up over half a dozen moves would be thrown away with one wild speculative dash across the board by her queen or one of her bishops. The inevitable losses of *matériel* that quickly followed would cause her to throw in rooks, knights and pawns in one glorious suicidal charge, each doomed piece being slammed down in a way that might have led a casual observer to believe that some grand plan lay behind the massacre and that the sole surviving bishop would miraculously achieve mate on its own. Then, when it was clear even to Geraldine that all was lost, she would sweep her fingers imperiously through the pieces, black and white, and demand another game. That the first game had not counted was taken as read. Geraldine always liked to start with a clean slate, however grubby she had made her previous one.

That was why none of the theories about Geraldine's disappearance could be entirely discounted by anyone who knew her well. The whole plan to abscond, the hired car, the suicide note – even at a pinch Geraldine tottering around West Wittering in red Italian high-heeled shoes – could all have been things which, for a moment or two, *simply looked like a good idea*. But equally one could not assume that everything had been done on a rash impulse. It was important to remember that the positions that she threw away had first to be built up. She was capable, when she chose, of careful, meticulous calculation and even, as a last resort, of sustained hard work.

Had I wanted to play detectives, and I most certainly did not, the one major advantage that I would have had over the police was a detailed knowledge of the character of Geraldine Tressider. Only Rupert, arguably, might have had a better one. But neither of us seemed to feel inclined, for the moment, to share that knowledge with those who were busy investigating Geraldine's murder.

On the day that Elsie took me for a stroll up to Cissbury Ring a further small part of the jigsaw was put in place. It was another phone call that placed this piece in my hands. This one was from Dickinson's – my wife's solicitors. They had at one time been mine and hers, but they handled the divorce on her behalf and relations between Tim Dickinson and myself had been somewhat distant ever since.

'Ethelred,' said the voice at the London end of the telephone. 'Good to talk to you again, though I would have preferred it was under other circumstances. I guess it was a while since you and Geraldine had seen each other, but my condolences, nevertheless. It must be tough for you.'

'Thank you for your condolences, Tim,' I said. 'How can I help you?'

'It's about Geraldine's will . . . slightly odd, but you still seem to be her executor, at least in the latest version that we have.'

'We made wills when we were still married. I guess that she never updated hers. She had no particular plans to die and so would not have given it a very high priority.'

'Yes . . . well, you remain the executor and the main beneficiary. Not, I fear, that you stand to inherit a great deal. Geraldine involved me quite closely in her business dealings and pretty well everything she had was security for one loan or another. And the business . . .'

'. . . was going down the plug hole.'

'Yes, you could put it like that. I assume you don't have a copy of the will?'

'Any reason why you think I should?'

'No, I suppose not. I'll send you a photocopy. You'll need to get access to the flat and so on; I'm not sure how.'

'I have keys,' I said. There was silence at the other end of the phone. 'It used to be my flat too,' I pointed out, 'until you took it away from me.'

'So it was,' he said. 'Now look, if we can be of any help in sorting out the estate or Geraldine's business affairs, please let me know.'

'Thank you. At a price, presumably.'

'I'm a solicitor,' he said. 'Everything is at a price. Ha ha. You might, however, like to think about it. We had a call from Mr Rupert Mackinnon, by the way, your late wife's . . . er . . . partner. He seemed to think that he should be the executor and indeed beneficiary of Geraldine's will.'

'Did he?'

'I'm only repeating what he told us.'

'I can see why he might think that.'

'If there's any doubt that there might be a later will somewhere naming Mr Mackinnon as executor we could always delay . . .'

'No,' I said. 'There's no other will and I'm the only executor.'

'If you're sure . . .'

'Quite sure,' I said.

Seven

Every wise man knows that there are occasions when it is inadvisable to tell his wife the entire truth. There are certain questions – 'How much did you have to drink last night?' 'How much did that cost?' 'Your new secretary's quite dishy, isn't she?' – that the alert husband will quickly realize may represent traps if answered in a frank and uninhibited fashion.

There is less need to dissemble to one's agent, though many authors I know seem to have problems with the question, 'Exactly when will the manuscript be ready?'

But one cannot lie to one's readers, particularly when it comes to crime writing. There is a standard of honesty to be maintained that runs strangely contrary to the murky subject matter. Above all, the reader must be given a fair chance to identify the murderer by (say) three-quarters of the way through the book, and the murderer cannot be some obscure character glimpsed briefly in chapter seven and never mentioned again.

This need for honesty occasionally runs against realism. For example, some of my more villainous characters, who would sell their own grandmothers, prove strangely incapable of telling a direct lie. When, for example, in *Thieves' Honour*, Ginger McVitie denies categorically that he paid Alf Jones to carry out a murder, the emphasis proves to be on the word 'paid': Jones has actually been *blackmailed* into carrying out the job. When my characters do tell a direct lie, they are usually offering the reader, in a quite generous fashion, the chance to spot an inconsistency between their statement and known facts.

This does not mean, of course, that one cannot lay endless trails of red herring in the path of the reader. As Geraldine had implied, these are, if not my stock in trade, at least a serviceable instrument that always sits in the toolbox of the crime writer. But they must be used with care to lead the reader off in a desired direction for a desired amount of time, not scattered randomly throughout the text. Nor are they the only tool in the box.

Clues must also obviously be provided: most openly, others half concealed in some throw-away line at the end of a section. I have sometimes been accused of providing too many clues too early on, but I am well aware that clues must be carefully doled out so that, while nobody can solve the mystery before the middle of the book, everyone has the chance of getting there before the final page.

But I do not necessarily treat all of my readers equally. I often, for example, throw in a line or two that will only be understandable to a tiny minority. I am by no means the only writer with such a penchant for private jokes. In *Enderby Outside* (page 94 of the Penguin edition) Anthony Burgess includes, with no attempt at explanation, a pun that could only be understood by a Malay speaker. Oddly enough, I was able to appreciate the joke, such as it is. During the first few months after Geraldine left me I found myself unable to write anything, other than one or two rather miserable and unpublishable poems. I was prescribed sleeping pills (most of which I still have stashed in the bathroom, for who knows what rainy day?) and I tried to forget other things by learning, first, Malay and then, later, some elementary Danish. I cannot say that either language has since been of immense benefit to me, but they both occupied my mind at a time when there was a large void to be occupied.

Finally, and more subtly, I like to include in my stories what I would describe as 'pointers'. These offer parallels to the main story, and suggest avenues that might be explored. In *All on a Summer's Day*, for example, where the interpretation of a date is critical to the plot, I have Sergeant Fairfax (in his capacity as an amateur historian) musing on a strange paradox: while the date of the first encounter between the Spanish Armada and the English fleet is beyond dispute, Spanish historians always give it as 31 July 1588, while their British counterparts more usually record it as 21 July. Why this anomaly for such a well-documented event? It is the sort of question, however, that I usually do not answer immediately, but leave hanging in the air for the reader to ponder. Occasionally I forget to explain it at all.

It did not surprise me that Elsie was in touch again soon after her visit to Findon. The reason for the call however was, ostensibly, routine literary business. A Danish publishing house wished to bring out a translation of *All on a Summer's Day*.

'Can't think why,' said Elsie, with her usual tact. 'I told them it was a crap book. Can't give it away here. And Danish sales won't bring in much money. Scarcely worth my time to set the deal up. But they seem to think that that gloomy, brooding sod Fairfax will appeal to the Nordic reader.'

'I wonder what they will call it in Danish,' I said. '*Hr. Fairfax' Fornemmelse for Datoer*, possibly.'

There was silence at the other end of the phone.

'Sorry – just a little private joke,' I said.

'Save it for your editor at Gyldendal,' she continued, after a short but meaningful silence. 'They're emailing me a contract. I assume the wonders of electronic communication are still unknown to you? I'll post you a copy when it arrives.'

'Don't worry. I'm coming up to London anyway on Tuesday. I have some things to clear up as Geraldine's executor.'

I knew it was a mistake to say this the moment the words had left my lips.

'What are you planning to do exactly?'

'Boring stuff. I need to look at the accounts of her business, check the flat, that sort of thing.'

'A chance to look for clues, though.'

'There will be no clues. This is dull stuff about the will. *Dull*, Elsie. Really uninteresting.'

'The flat is in Barnsbury Street, isn't it? I still have your old address somewhere. I'll meet you there at eleven on Tuesday.'

'Elsie . . .'

But the phone had already been put down at the other end.

Bugger.

Eight

When I moved from Islington to Sussex, it was a form of self-imposed exile. In part, it is true, there were financial considerations that obliged me to move. And there was a straightforward desire to put as many miles as I could between Geraldine and myself. But it was also an act of contrition – a recognition that I had failed to hold together the only marriage I had ever had and that I deserved to live in the outer darkness, only just this side of Worthing.

I had expected, on my first visit to Islington for many years, to see some changes. But the neat terraces of narrow but expensive Georgian houses still shone in the shafting sunshine, each front door painted in authentic heritage hues – Oxford blue, walnut brown, claret, Brunswick green – the quiet, confident colours of money. The rows of railings fronting both sides of the street were a glossy jet black. Autumn was sliding in unobtrusively: not a Findon riot of golds and reds, but the leaves of the carefully spaced cherry trees had on them the merest hint of burnt orange – one of that year's fashionable colours.

Elsie was waiting for me at the street door, tapping her size 3 foot and raring to go. Today's unsuitable outfit for the smaller woman proved to be a yellow trouser suit with large red checks, and I hoped that she would not ask me if it made her bottom look big.

'Nice suit,' I observed defensively, as she handed me my copy of the Gyldendal contract. 'New?'

'You took your sodding time,' she replied, temporarily shelving the bottom question.

'I had to come from Sussex. You only had to come from Hampstead.'

'I'm a woman. I'm not supposed to be on time. You're a man. You're meant to be here to let me in. It's a thing men do.'

'The age of chivalry has been dead for some time. Since 1485 men have done pretty much as they pleased. Blame Henry VII.'

'Don't be a silly tosser, Tressider,' Elsie observed. And I let her into the flat.

Once through the door, Elsie bustled round like a fat little terrier, almost literally sniffing the air for clues. 'You take the sitting room, I'll check the bedroom,' she said.

'You take whichever room you like,' I said. 'I need to get papers together for probate.'

She snorted at my lack of enthusiasm for what she considered to be the real business in hand, but waddled off to the bedroom, where for a while she could be heard opening cupboards and nosing through whatever least belonged to her.

I was happy to have a few minutes to myself. I quickly

found the relevant files. They were still in the same drawer that they had occupied when I lived in the flat, and indeed many still had my handwriting on the cover. I extracted the recent statements from the file marked 'BANK'. A swift glance revealed that there was little to give comfort to any of Geraldine's creditors. I was also able to locate something else I needed, in an old chocolate box that had served for many years as a receptacle for spare keys. By the time Elsie emerged triumphantly from the bedroom and started her investigation of the sitting room, I had almost finished my own work.

'So, what have you come up with?' she demanded.

'Only papers on Geraldine's finances.'

'Skint?'

'In a manner of speaking. A small positive balance on her current account.'

'Building societies? Shares?'

'Building society account closed. No shares that I can find. Large mortgage, recently increased, but the sale of the flat should cover that. Unpaid creditors from her previous exploits, who will never see their money now. Ditto credit cards, I fear.'

'Pretty much as expected then.'

'Pretty much,' I conceded.

'So, you've discovered nothing. Typical. Come and see what I've found,' she said, smirking.

She led me into the bedroom and threw open a wardrobe door.

'There!' she said. 'That is not a woman's wardrobe.'

I looked at the row of dresses and skirts hanging neatly from the rail.

'You don't see what I mean, do you?' she said. She waved an empty coat hanger at me. 'What's this then?'

'An empty coat hanger?' I hazarded.

'Exactly!' she exclaimed.

'I don't follow.'

'You're a man,' she reminded me for the second time that morning.

'Sorry,' I said.

'A woman's wardrobe,' she said, very slowly and carefully, 'does not have empty hangers. A woman's wardrobe is crammed full, because it contains the clothes you actually wear and it also contains all sorts of other things that you have bought over the years and kept because you never know when you might wake up one morning as a perfect size ten again. OK? This wardrobe is only two-thirds full, which means that half of the clothes have gone.'

Ignoring for a moment the strange mathematics of women's wardrobes, I surveyed the contents and admitted that it was less full than I remembered it.

'So, she had time to pack,' said Elsie. 'That's two or three suitcases. Where are they now? They weren't in the car. And come and look at this.'

She led me back to the sitting room and stood me in front of the bookcase. 'What do you see? And don't say "books" or I'll have to cut your dick off with a rusty hacksaw.'

I stayed silent. It seemed like the safest option.

'See those little yellow dots?'

I nodded. I had in fact noticed them earlier, but had said nothing to Elsie. They were small, removable sticky-backed paper circles, attached quite inconspicuously to the spines of some of the books and to the photo albums. 'So?' I enquired.

'Well,' said Elsie, 'they're what you put on things when you move house, so that the removal men will know where to take them. You know: blue dots for the sitting room, green triangles for the dining room, white squares for the main bedroom, pink stars for the kitchen, yellow dots—'

'I get the picture,' I said.

'So, why the yellow dots?' Elsie persisted. 'She was doing a runner. She wasn't going to get the removal men to come in and crate things up for her.'

'Maybe they had some other purpose entirely.'

'Hang on,' Elsie announced suddenly. 'Look – there's one on that watercolour too.' She started prowling round the room on a serious dot-hunt. 'And on this vase. And on this photo frame.'

'Red herring,' I said. 'They're probably from when she and Rupert split up. Maybe she was marking things that were hers and that Rupert was not to take. Somewhere in Rupert's new flat there are probably rows of books with green pentagons on them.'

'That's possible,' said Elsie, crestfallen.

'I wouldn't worry about it,' I said.

'Still, it does at least confirm that she had been planning her departure. You don't pack three cases for a suicide. She had definite plans to go somewhere and to look smart when she got there. And where are the cases now, eh?' demanded Elsie.

'Where indeed?' I asked.

'So, what next?' Elsie asked briskly.

'Next I have to visit the bank,' I said. 'And you are on your way back to Hampstead.

'No buts, Elsie. Thanks for bringing the contract down – I'm grateful. For the next couple of hours however I have to look like an executor, and an apprentice detective at my heels will not be required.'

Elsie haggled a bit and, as a concession, I agreed in my capacity as executor that she could raid the kitchen for any chocolate that Geraldine might have left behind.

'Well, she won't be needing it wherever she is,' said Elsie.

'Where she is, it would probably melt,' I said.

It is rarely necessary to lie to one's agent, but in this case I had been a little economical with the truth. I had for example not one but a number of visits that I wanted to pay without Elsie's running commentary in the background. The first was only a few hundred yards away, and required the keys that I had located in the ex-chocolate box.

Standing in the pigeon droppings and old newspapers at street level, I was able to confirm that I had reached my destination by means of a small sign attached to the wall of a nondescript fifties industrial building: 'Geraldine Tressider (Property Division) 3rd Floor'. It was unclear, as with so much that she did, why occupying part of this grimy concrete-and-plate-glass eyesore on a noisy main road had appealed to Geraldine as part of her business strategy. The other identifiable occupants were a casting agency and a firm classifying itself as 'import-export', though what it imported and what it exported was not specified. The street door proved to be unlocked and, since there was no lift, I climbed the three flights of unswept stairs to Geraldine's Corporate Headquarters.

Once inside the office, it was evident that what Geraldine had been saving on rent, she had allocated to furnishings. In the larger, starkly white, outer office, there were comfortable modern chairs upholstered in black leather, and a large curving desk with a new computer on it. Suspiciously pristine, almost certainly empty, bright red box files and some reference books were carefully spaced on well-polished wood-and-steel shelving. On an oval coffee table rested the current editions of two or three glossy magazines. The leaves of the obligatory office plant gleamed as though they had been oiled. Post lay neatly stacked in an in-tray. Only the lack of any human activity spoiled the air of quiet efficiency. The inner office – Geraldine's sanctum – was a repeat of this on a smaller scale, with cherry-wood blinds to hide the uninspiring view of the buildings across the road and a small green Buddha sitting Elsie-like, fat and self-satisfied, on a low corner table.

I knew what I needed and, as had happened at the flat, it took only a short time to locate what passed for Geraldine's financial records. They confirmed what was becoming a consistent story: the company had no assets to speak of. I was just trying to decide whether to undertake a more thorough search of the office when I heard a key in the lock. Just for a moment I had a vision of Geraldine waltzing through the door as if nothing had happened, then the improbability of this struck me and I sprang to my feet.

I emerged from the inner office just in time to see a pimply young man, hands occupied with a carton of milk and cheap plastic document case, in the process of trying to close the front door with his elbow. He turned, saw me, gasped, let go of the milk, grabbed it again as it reached waist height, juggled with it for a couple of seconds and dropped the document holder.

'Shit!' he said. Then he yielded to the inevitable and dropped the milk too.

'Who the hell are you?' I asked.

He ignored my enquiry. 'What are you doing here?'

I ignored his. 'I asked you first.'

He paused. This pattern of questioning was likely to occupy us for most of the day unless one of us changed tack. 'I'm Darren. Darren Oxtoby. I work for Mrs Tressider – worked, I mean. I'm her assistant. Was.'

'Ethelred Tressider,' I said. 'My ex-wife's executor.'

'Right,' he said uncertainly. He picked up the milk carton, which fortunately had not burst on impact.

He was recovering from the shock of finding somebody in what should have been an empty office. I, of course, should not have been shocked to see him: the carefully piled post in the tray, the new magazines, the watered plants should all have told me that the office was continuing to operate after a fashion – quite possibly more efficiently than when Geraldine had been present in person. Perhaps it should always have occurred to me that Geraldine would have employed staff of some sort – half-witted charity cases, almost certainly. After all, it would not have been possible to achieve the sort of losses she usually sustained single-handed. But for some reason I had not pictured this gangly young man with a spotty face and a tendency to perform vaudeville acts with milk cartons. If I was ignorant of his existence, then in all likelihood the police also were. But did he know anything of value?

'All right,' I said. 'Where is she?'

His eyes widened and his jaw dropped open. For a moment I thought that he was about to do the milk trick again, and I was not sure that the carton would survive a second drop.

'But . . .' he said. 'But . . . she's *dead*.'

If he had not had the desk behind him, I think he would have tried to back away from me as a dangerous lunatic.

'Not Geraldine,' I said with some show of justifiable irritation. 'For God's sake – I am scarcely expecting to see Geraldine here, am I? Where is Charlotte?'

'Who?'

'Charlotte Turner. Geraldine's sister. Isn't she supposed to be a partner here?'

'Miss Turner? She doesn't come here. She's a – what do you call it? – sleeping partner. I've spoken to her on the phone, but I've never met her.'

'Has she phoned since Geraldine disappeared?'

'Once. I just said that I didn't know where Mrs Tressider was. It was what I was always supposed to say to people.' The spotty one shrugged his bony shoulders.

'So Geraldine – Mrs Tressider – didn't tell Miss Turner where she was planning to go?'

'She can't have done, can she? Or why would Miss Turner have asked me?'

'No,' I said. 'I suppose not. And what did Mrs Tressider tell you?'

'Nothing. Not really. She just said that she wouldn't be in for a while and to tell people she would get in touch with them when she got back.'

'So she didn't say where she was going?'

'Switzerland. I think she had some sort of deal lined up there.'

'Are you sure?'

'Yes. Come to think of it she didn't actually *tell* me where she was going but I overheard her making the booking. I'd said I could do it, but she said, no, I should get on with my other work. I don't remember the tickets arriving though – maybe she picked them up herself.'

'And what is the other work that Mrs Tressider said you should get on with?'

'I do some filing. I make coffee sometimes. I answer the phone.'

'I suppose that's what they call "multi-tasking" in the job adverts.'

'Sorry?'

'Nothing. So did Mrs Tressider keep you busy?'

He laughed. 'No, not really. I spend a lot of time working on my book.' He pointed to the cheap plastic wallet. 'I'm going to be a writer.' He smiled diffidently.

'Really? That's a coincidence. I've just spent most of the morning with a literary agent,' I said.

His eyes opened wide. 'A literary agent. Gosh!' he said. 'Do you know an *agent*?'

'Yes,' I said. 'Very well, unfortunately.'

'Do you think you could introduce me to her?'

'Yes,' I said. 'I certainly could, but I am afraid I'm not

going to. Sorry about that. Now, how long have you been here?'

'I've just arrived. You saw me come in.'

'I mean when did you start working here?'

'Oh, I see. About three months ago.'

'I didn't see any mention of you in the books.'

'Books?'

'The accounts,' I said. 'There's nothing to say that any staff are being employed. No salary. No National Insurance. No tax. Mrs Tressider was paying you?'

'Oh yes, every week. Cash.'

And no questions asked. That would have been Geraldine all right. But why? He was clearly superfluous to the non-business that she was running.

'So why are you still coming in?'

He shrugged. 'I use the computer to type my novel.'

'Well, not any more, you don't. As of today this office is closed. If you leave a note of your name and address, I'll see you get sent a week's pay in lieu of notice – if the company has any assets to pay you from. I'll have your key back too, before you go.'

He looked thoroughly miserable.

'Couldn't I just come in to use the computer? Nobody else needs it.'

'No,' I said. 'Oh, and one other thing. Have the police contacted you?'

'Not yet.'

'Well, I'd stay out of their way. You know that you've been working here illegally without tax and National Insurance?

I think that it would be best if they did not know about that, don't you?'

He looked even more miserable. I've never beaten a puppy – in that respect I had a rather deprived childhood – but he looked rather as I imagine a beaten puppy might look.

'I'll leave the key then,' he said.

'Just pull the door to when you go. I've got work to do.'

And I returned to the inner office to contemplate what passed for Geraldine's accounts.

I knew perfectly well that I had treated Darren badly, and I was not especially proud of the way I had behaved. But why had I taken such an instant and profound dislike to him? He was, after all, a harmless, if rather awkward, young man. He merely wished to get on with his novel and not disturb anyone in the process. If he had a slightly exalted idea of the status of a novelist (and a very much exalted idea of the status of a literary agent), I could scarcely hold that against him. Then it occurred to me. Of course – bright-eyed, eager, shy, gangly and with an almost pathetic desire to please – he precisely resembled me at the same age.

So, that was OK then. He had deserved all that he got.

Nine

There is an important difference between fiction and real life. Fiction has to be believable.

The novelist is obliged to have his small cast act in character, ignoring the fact that we are all a mass of exceptions and contradictions. In real life no sooner have we categorized somebody as miserly, than they disappoint us with some totally unnecessary act of generosity. In real life the most unlikely people become heroes, and people that you would walk past in the street without a second glance may have a murdered grandmother buried beneath the concrete floor of the new conservatory.

Geraldine however stretched to the limits even real life's capacity for the capricious and unexpected. Her sudden changes of tack, her ability to contradict one minute what she had confidently stated the minute before, made little sense when considered from day to day or week to week. It was only when you were able to take a longer-term view that you saw that her life was like an impressionist painting. Close to it was a series of random splodges of colour – very pretty, but not adding up to much more than that. It was only when you stood back that you were obliged to gasp at the daring and supreme economy of effort in the grand plan.

But what was the grand plan this time? For a moment I thought that I had caught a glimpse of it. Now I had begun to wonder whether that grey smudge was a boat or a cloud on the horizon. And was that figure in the foreground turning towards me or away from me? I needed to step back a little further, and question some of the things that I had taken for granted.

My next stop that autumn morning was at a bank on Upper Street. Geraldine had abused it for many years, both for her business and private banking. I too had been a customer in the days when we were together.

I suppose there would have been a time when, under these circumstances, I might have expected to have been met personally by the bank manager and offered condolences. I was not surprised however to be met by a young lady with a large file and a clipboard that she checked from time to time to remind herself of my name.

'I have prepared these papers for you to sign, Mr . . . um . . . Tressider,' she announced nasally. 'They will enable us to set up an executor's account for you, into which we can transfer your wife's assets.'

'Which are relatively modest.'

'But in credit.' She smiled. My wife was dead but she was in credit, which would be a great comfort to me.

'So, it's all straightforward from your point of view?' I asked.

'Perfectly. As Mrs . . . um . . . Tressider's executor you are however aware that there may be funds of hers in Switzerland?'

'Really?'

'Well, we're not terribly sure, but there were two large transfers from her personal account to an account in Geneva. I had assumed that you would know about it.'

'I'm sure it is all quite in order,' I said.

She smiled. 'That's what we had hoped.'

I signed the papers.

'Thank you Mr . . . um . . . Tressider,' she said.

I had already gathered together my papers and shaken her hand when the phone next to her rang.

'Yes, Mr Smith, we're just tying everything up now. No, Mr . . . um . . . Tressider is about to leave. Yes, certainly, I'll ask him.' She turned to me. 'The manager would like to see you, if you have a few minutes.'

I looked at my watch. 'A few minutes?' I said. 'Why not?'

I had met Smith, the manager, before, in the days when he had watched over our minimalist joint savings and our quite substantial joint mortgage. I had good cause to remember him for all sorts of reasons, but, as with Rupert, I failed for a brief instant to recognize the plump figure behind the mahogany desk, though I would have been hard put to say in exactly what ways he had changed. At all events, he now looked very much like the bank manager he was: of medium height, rapidly thickening waist and gradually receding hairline, disguised for the moment by none-too-skilful sideways combing. His lips were of the rather prominent variety that can sometimes look full and sensuous in youth, but which become increasingly flabby and unattractive with age. His skin was distinctly oily. His suit, a cheap but still new-looking grey chalk-stripe, was easily the most presentable part of him. He seemed both to have remembered me and to have forgotten our last painful interview some ten years before, because he greeted me with a firm handshake and a sympathetic smile. Perhaps, after all, these old-fashioned niceties had not been completely forgotten.

'Ethelred . . . my condolences. Terrible business. *Terrible* business. Coffee?'

He poured me a cup from a pot that was sitting on a warming device on a side table. I had not been offered coffee the last time we had met.

'Thank you,' I said. 'I've already been through things with your assistant. I'm told that everything is in order.'

He coughed, and he took a sip of coffee. For a moment a gossamer thread of spittle joined his thick lips to the cup. 'I hope so,' he said. He spoke slowly and carefully, with a slight Scottish accent, dwelling unexpectedly on certain words as if for emphasis. 'Yes, I *do* hope *so*.'

'But the account is in credit?'

'Oh, yes. In *credit*. Oh, *certainly*. Unfortunately she also has quite a large loan outstanding, and no trace of funds to cover it.'

'Sorry – was there another account that I have missed?'

'Not another account, no. Not another *account* as such. But she did owe a great deal of *money*.'

'How much?'

'Three hundred thousand pounds.'

'I see.'

'It appears that she transferred this and some other money to Switzerland shortly before she . . . er . . . died. I need to recover it. Or rather I need you as *executor* to do this for us.'

'You know where the money is then?'

'We know the bank, but they are, being a *Swiss* bank, reluctant to divulge details about the account. We believe that your wife had an account with them into which she transferred the funds in question. It is unlikely that she could have done very much with the money before her death, and so it is presumably still there. Its recovery should be a relatively simple task – for you.'

'Will it indeed?'

'I shall obviously offer you what help I can.'

'I'm surprised that the bank was willing to lend her so much, given her past record. What did she offer as security?'

'Yes. Well, there lies the problem. She did not offer any *security* for the loan.'

'And the bank gave her the money? You've changed your policy since I banked with you.'

'Ah. There lies the other problem. The *bank*'s policy has not changed at all.'

'You've lost me.'

'*I* gave her the money, Ethelred. Me. It was a personal loan. The *bank* was not involved. I sold shares to raise the sum.'

'But why?'

'I must admit that it does now appear a foolish move on

my part, but the proposition that she put forward offered a *very* high rate of return. I had only intended to leave the money with her for a short time before *reinvesting* it.'

'I see.'

'I need to reinvest as soon as I can.' He took a quick sip of coffee.

'Before the stock market rises?'

'Before my wife finds out. I had not told her of this particular plan. She may feel, with hindsight, that it was a little *unwise*.' He gave a little nervous laugh and a conspiratorial glance. One husband to another (ex-) husband. 'So, you really *do* have to help me.'

I smiled back and said nothing.

He looked at me uncertainly. 'Are you saying that you can't . . . *won't* help me?'

I in turn took another sip of coffee, but very slowly, then replaced the cup carefully on the saucer.

'I shall need all the facts,' I said.

'Of course,' he said, with a gasp of relief. 'The *facts*. Of *course*.'

He provided me there and then with a small sheaf of papers, promising to phone the remaining details through as soon as he could.

As I left the office I felt that another small piece of Geraldine's grand design had been fitted into place, but exactly what the piece was remained unclear. A boat? A cloud? Only time would tell.

I had one final visit to pay, following up a telephone call I had made earlier that day. In a side street of narrow red-brick houses, just off the Holloway Road, rain was streaking the grime of long-unwashed windows. There was no need to push the gate open: years of unchecked wet rot had made sure that it would never close again. A long pause followed my pressing the fourth-floor bell, then I heard slippered feet descending the stairs. The door opened a few inches and Rupert's face appeared briefly round the edge. It closed, I heard a chain being removed, and the door finally juddered open again.

'Thank goodness. Do you have any news?'

'I'm more worried about the weather forecast than the news,' I said. 'I'm getting absolutely soaked. You might just let me in.'

'I'm frightfully sorry,' he said. 'Come on up, then tell me.'

As he led me up the seemingly endless flights of stairs, it struck me that the seediness of his new surroundings had started to rub off on him. The corduroy trousers were old, the jersey had only one elbow rather than the normal number, and he had not shaved.

The flat was small and had all the marks of being a temporary staging post on his route to wherever it was he was going. The botched paintwork, the ill-fitting chair covers, the stained rug, the dusty Indian blinds suggested that few of the previous tenants had planned to stay there long either. It was bad enough, but even from here you could of course still go down. Down is one way you can always go.

'I have less news than I would like,' I began. 'It won't surprise you to learn that there is no money in Geraldine's account.'

'But my two hundred thousand?'

'Gone to Switzerland,' I said.

I watched his expression carefully, but it betrayed nothing except blank incomprehension. 'Switzerland? Why?'

'It's where all money would go if it had the choice. It's where money is loved and appreciated. You mean you didn't know that she was planning to move the money overseas?'

He shook his head as if at some impossibly difficult crossword question. 'To Switzerland? No. I've told you: she was planning to invest it in some houses in Hackney. What would be the point of transferring it to Switzerland? Look, Ethelred, I have just got to get that money back.'

'Which is why I am continuing my researches. The bank is getting me details of the account. If it is in her name it may not be too difficult for me to retrieve the money.'

'It might not be in her name? Why do you think that?'

'Let's not worry about that yet,' I said quickly, though if he was not worried at this stage then he never would be. Or perhaps he could be a tad more concerned if he knew about Smith's little loan to Geraldine, which would complicate the ownership of anything that might be recoverable. I could have told him, of course. But I didn't.

'I'm terribly grateful to you, Ethelred. You don't know how reassuring it is to know that you are looking after things.'

'We go back a long way,' I said with a friendly smile. 'But perhaps you can give me a little more help?'

'Anything. Just ask.'

'Over the past year did you ever get the feeling that there was somebody else in her life?'

'Before we split up or after?'

'Both.' There had been something that he was planning to tell me that evening at my flat in Findon. Perhaps he would choose to reveal more now.

'I'm not really in a position to comment on after, but before – yes, certainly. Since about March, if I had to put a date on it. Nothing I could really put my finger on – just that she would be away for odd days, or sometimes overnight. She said that she was also looking at various projects outside London, which she may well have been, of course.'

'But it made you suspicious?'

'No . . . well, yes. There was one occasion when she said she had been to Leeds. Then, when I borrowed the car a couple of days later, I found one of those car park tickets on the dashboard. It was for the day that she said she had been in Leeds, but it was for a car park in Chichester.'

'Careless,' I said.

'I mean: Leeds . . . Chichester . . . it would have all been the same to me, so why tell me one when she was at the other? Then of course six months later her car turns up at West Wittering, not half a dozen miles from Chichester.'

'Coincidence?'

'Maybe. That's why I wondered . . . you live down that way . . . did she ever call in to see you . . . about last May, it would have been.'

'Why should she do that?' I asked.

'No, of course not. Silly of me to ask. But it did make me think at the time.'

'Was there anything else? That made you suspicious, I mean.'

He frowned and then shook his head. 'No,' he said with

a sigh. 'Just that she was away a lot and sometimes appeared . . . I don't know . . . distracted. And it isn't that I haven't thought about it. I suppose I might feel better about all this if she had left me for another man. But in the end she just left me. I had expected her, once we split up, to move straight in with somebody else. But she never did.'

'Does the name Darren Oxtoby mean anything to you?'

'Darren? He was the gormless office boy she took on.'

'So there was nothing going on there?'

'Darren?' He laughed out loud. I had really managed to cheer him up, it seemed. My journey had not after all been totally in vain. 'Darren? Good God, no. Not even in my wildest extremes of jealousy could I have supposed that Geraldine would be attracted to Darren. Could you?'

'No,' I said quickly. 'No, I couldn't. Forget I said it. And there was nobody else?'

'Like I said: I really don't know. There could have been. I knew what I was taking on with Geraldine. That was why we split up all those years ago at Oxford of course; her attention tended to wander unless you watched her closely. You must have had the same problem.'

'Other men? While she was married to me? I don't think so,' I said. 'Except for you, obviously.'

'But . . .' He gave me a funny sort of look that I couldn't quite account for, then shrugged. 'Whatever you say, old man. How is this important anyway? Do you think that she was planning to run off with somebody?'

'I honestly don't know either,' I said. But the piece of the jigsaw next to the grey smudge was now in place. And it was a boat all right. It was a boat.

All the way back to Findon the rain splattered against the windscreen. The traffic crawled through the seedy, puddled byways of Clapham and Wandsworth. The road danced in my headlights, the glimmering surface in a constant state of agitation. I arrived back tired and ready only for a whisky and bed.

I parked the car in my appointed space and was irritated to see, as I walked back, one of the girls from the village sitting on the wall in front of Greypoint House, kicking at the flints with her heels. I gave her a frown. 'I don't think that's your wall to kick,' I observed.

She looked up and squinted at me. 'What's it to you?'

'It happens to be my wall,' I said. 'At least, one-eighth of it is.'

'One-eighth? Of *this*?'

'Roughly.'

'Get a life,' she observed, and gave the wall a good hard bang with her heel before jumping down.

I scowled again and said, 'And don't let me catch you there again' – or something equally middle-aged and ineffectual.

But what I was thinking was this. 'A life? Yes, that's not a bad idea. One of these days I really must get one of those.'

Ten

If there's one thing that gets up my sodding nose, it's starting a new chapter and finding that the poxy narrator has changed. Changing the typeface just adds insult to injury, as if the author (silly tosser) reckons the reader won't recognize it's somebody else without double underlining everything and putting it in twenty-four-point sodding Haettenschweiler. Or whatever.

It was the sort of trick that I had to warn Ethelred against in the way that mothers used to warn their sons against scarlet women. Mind you, I should have warned Ethelred about women as well, before the Bitch got her claws into him. I was onto her game from day one. Oh yes. But you can't make people see. Not when they imagine they're in love. I'd pass a law against it myself.

When the Bitch cleared off, it almost destroyed him. For months he wrote nothing, which is fine if you've got royalties from a dozen books coming in, but he hadn't. And I don't need to tell you what my 12½ per cent of sod all was. He even let the Bitch have the flat and anything else she wanted.

Nobody seemed to be on his side in those days. His best friend had stuffed him. His sister-in-law, Charlotte, had never really liked him – she regarded Ethelred as a dead loss from the start: a lanky, mournful loser unworthy even of her sister. When they split up she could, initially, scarcely contain her glee. (It was only later, when she got to know Rupert better, that she realized that Geraldine could have done worse than Ethelred.) His bank manager – a guy named Smith, whom he'd known for years – even turned him down for a mortgage on the basis that his writer's income alone was insufficient security. That more than anything else forced Ethelred out of London, away from his friends and down into the depths of Sussex, where living was cheaper and bank managers more understanding. Since most of his former friends seemed to be lining up to kick him, moving out of their reach was not, perhaps, the unmitigated disaster it might have been. Not, as far as I could tell, that he made any new friends down by the sea. He didn't seem willing to trust anyone. Nobody. Ever.

So, when Ethelred moved to Findon I thought, right, he's broke, he's screwed up, he's got no mates, but at least the Bitch is out of his hair.

For a while the books flowed nicely again. A regular Fairfax every year, building up a nice loyal readership. When he wanted to try something different – historical stuff – I suggested he did so under another name, and that worked too. So did the romantic fiction – though it was obviously, like all romantic fiction, a load of old bollocks.

When did it start going wrong? Before the Bitch's death, certainly. I noticed a sort of restlessness, a reluctance to get down to the next Fairfax, which even then was overdue. He kept saying why didn't he try this and why didn't he try that? Because you're not up to it, you silly tart, I would reply. Well, you have to be cruel to be kind sometimes, don't you?

Then he went off to France and I thought, OK, so maybe the change will do him some good. But it was worse after that. Her death affected him oddly – and I mean oddly.

Take the evening we heard she'd gone missing. (I generously hung around and sat with him in case the pigs gave him a hard time.) He didn't turn a hair when the copper said that she'd committed suicide. He did say, 'Bloody hell,' or something when he heard she'd done it at West Wittering. But what really seemed to upset him was the fact that she'd been driving a red Fiat. I mean, how does any of that add up?

Then there were times when you could have sworn that he didn't give a damn whether the murderer was caught or not. Again, don't get me wrong here: my own attitude was a little ambivalent, shall we say? Whoever had murdered Geraldine had obviously done so with the best of intentions, and there was no point in trying to blame anyone. But I was curious to know who had done it. Well, you are, aren't you?

So there was Ethelred dashing from place to place asking everyone questions. (And don't tell me that was just to fulfil his duties as an executor. I mean, do me a favour.) But he didn't seem interested in actually finding anything out. And he seemed neither properly miserable nor jubilant at the Bitch's untimely demise.

He'd only ever really loved two women, he once told me. One was this teacher he'd had at primary school, the other was the Bitch. And both, strangely, had been called Geraldine. So, I could have understood if he'd been a bit upset, even after all this time, at something happening to one or other of them. But he wasn't.

On the other hand, he *was* worried about something. I noticed it first … when? Just after he had identified the body. Distressing no doubt, but, in a way, it should have been cathartic. I mean it might have triggered the self-pitying remorse or it might have cheered him up a bit. But that was exactly when he started to become moody, bad-tempered almost. And worried. Yes, definitely worried.

And the whole time I felt that there was stuff he knew, but he didn't want to tell me. Does that make sense to you? I mean, does it make sense his not telling *me*?

So what was Ethelred's great quest all about? I knew of course that after his visit to the flat he'd been to Geraldine's old office, then to the bank, then to see Rupert. I wasn't supposed to know that? Oh, give me some credit for a *bit* of deviousness. No, I didn't follow him . . . well, all right, I did follow him for a bit, but once he set off up the Holloway Road, I knew that a quick phone call later would confirm whether or not he'd been to see Rupert. Not bad for an apprentice, eh?

So I sat by the phone that evening waiting for him to call and tell me what he'd found out, but did he? Nothing for it in that case but to drive down to Findon, on a plausible pretext that I would come up with in due course, and pay him a visit. Little did I imagine that the visit would be quite as profitable as it was.

Eleven

It rained for most of the next week, and then it carried on raining. I later read that it had been the wettest autumn since records began. All that morning I had sat in front of my computer trying to conjure up a new Fairfax story, but the rain dripped and dripped from the broken gutter above the window and Fairfax remained sulky and uncommunicative. Several times I got off to what seemed to be a good start, but on each occasion I found the storyline taking an odd, almost surreal direction. Fairfax had in the past often expressed a contempt for all types of detective fiction, ignoring the fact that he was himself a product of the genre. Now it was as if he had suddenly woken up to the strange anomaly of his position and was mocking me. Twice I completed over a thousand words before deleting the whole thing and starting again.

My third attempt was interrupted by another visit from the police. I had had little contact with them for a week or so, but now they seemed anxious to brief me on their progress.

'We think, Mr Tressider, that we have been able to link your wife's murder to a number of others in the area.'

'I see.'

'There have been four killings over the past two years that we believe are connected. All of the victims were female and blonde, all were strangled, and their bodies were all found within twenty miles or so of where we discovered your wife. There was also a further incident – another blonde lady. She got talking to a man in a pub and he then offered to drive her home. Said he had a Porsche, which indeed he did. As they drove along, however, she became aware that the route he was taking was not the most direct one. They stopped and he suggested a moonlight stroll, but she was understandably cautious at this stage and on her guard. When he confirmed her suspicions by trying to strangle her, she kneed him in the groin and, to cut a long story short, we now have a very good description of him. I am pleased to say that as a result we think we have made a positive identification.'

'And you have made an arrest?' I was suddenly quite literally on the edge of my seat.

'Not yet. He has disappeared. Gone. Scarpered.'

No reply seemed to be expected of me, so I said nothing.

'We're going to run the case on *Crimewatch*,' he added with more than a hint of pride. 'No harm in telling you who he is, since we'll be asking for information on him then. Does the name George Peters mean anything to you?'

'No,' I said, finally able to trust myself to speak. Even going back to my earliest childhood I honestly couldn't think of anyone I had met named George Peters.

'Well, that's our man,' he said, 'and once we pull him in,

I don't think we'll have to look much further for your wife's killer.'

'Well done,' I said.

'You don't sound convinced,' he said.

'No, I really am frightfully impressed, officer.'

He squinted at me. 'If there is anything that you know about the murder that you haven't told us, sir, I would advise you to do so. Withholding evidence could be an offence.'

I leaned back in my chair and stretched out my legs. 'Why on earth would I do that?' I said.

After the police had left, I felt that I had to get out, even if I got soaked to the skin in the process, but the skies brightened towards the end of the morning, and the rain became no more than an intermittent drizzle. Accordingly I donned a Barbour and wellingtons and set off along Nepcote Lane and up towards Cissbury Ring.

The steady rain had started to strip the trees of their leaves and abandon them in soggy black drifts on each side of the road. There they formed miniature dams, holding back lateral puddles of murky water. The last sad blackberries of a poor season hung grey and rotting on the bare branches. The sheep looked damp and miserable. And water dripped and dripped. It did little else. From every branch, every leaf, every twig, it dripped.

I skirted the Ring and pressed on across the downs in the direction of Steyning. The chalky mud was often the consistency of wet cement, but out here in the clean upland air, problems that had seemed immense dwindled into the blue distance. I had frequently found that a long walk enabled me to get ideas clear in my mind and to resolve inconsistencies that had suddenly revealed themselves in the plot.

Today was no exception and, in the damp autumn Sussex countryside, I forgot such troubles as I had seemed to have and started to see a picture of a sultry summer's evening in Buckford.

Fairfax is sitting at his desk. He is once more contemplating retirement. And he is deeply troubled, though it is not yet clear about what. He is talking to one of the younger policemen – apparently about everyday matters, but increasingly hinting to the reader some inner conflict that will undoubtedly be revealed in later chapters. We cut to another part of Buckford. A man is contemplating a crime, though we do not yet know what the crime is. This is not however some ordinary villain – this is somebody well known to Fairfax, a friend, to the extent that Fairfax has friends. At some point his story and Fairfax's are destined to converge, but not for several chapters. Events, whatever they prove to be, will test Fairfax's loyalties to the utmost. Or then again perhaps not. Perhaps he will have no difficulty in bringing this friend to justice. Perhaps he will abandon his loyalties to a service that has signally failed to reward him for his efforts. Perhaps it will be his very last case.

What happens next? I don't yet know. But the story has started flowing. And this small trickle may gather pace and become a stream, then a torrent that will carry the story off, who knows where? But that hot summer night would be the starting point.

The sun broke through the clouds as I passed Cissbury Ring on my return. In the warmer air steam was rising distinctly from the backs of the sheep. Here and there dry patches were appearing on the road. On Nepcote Green, Catrin from Findon Farmhouse was out walking Thistle, her Border terrier. I gave her a wave as usual and she waved back. Somewhere a bird, in its ignorance, may possibly have sung. Is it only with hindsight that I feel that everything on that walk back was suspiciously normal? That I was being lulled into a false sense of security?

Greypoint House too looked its usual self, though the gutter was still dripping gently onto the gravel below. I climbed the stairs to my flat, eager to sit down again in front of the keyboard. Fat chance of that.

The first sign I had that anything was amiss was the fact that the mortice on my front door was unlocked, whereas I was certain that I had locked it when I left. Cautiously I turned the key in the Yale, and opened the door. I paused, carefully reached for a walking stick from the stand by the door and listened, then (hoping for an element of surprise) I sprang into the sitting room.

Elsie looked up from where she was sitting. 'What are you playing at, Ethelred, you tart?'

In front of her, spread out on my coffee table, were all of Geraldine's accounts. On the floor for some reason was a book of road maps of the British Isles. Clutched in her hand was a bar of chocolate. Seeing my frown of displeasure she looked first at the chocolate, then at the accounts and then back to the chocolate.

'Oh, for goodness' sake,' she said. 'It was in the *cupboard*.'

Twelve

I parked my car just round the corner from Greypoint House and walked over and rang the bell. No sodding reply, of course. You'd have thought that even Ethelred would have had the sense not to go out on a day when it was pissing down, but there you are.

Then I had my first little stroke of good luck. (Oh yes, there were to be others.) The front door opened and this old biddy said, 'Can I help you, dearie?'

'I was looking for Ethelred Tressider, but it seems as though he's gone out.'

'Oh, he's just gone out for a walk. I doubt he'll be back for an hour at least. I've got his spare key. Why don't I let you in, so that you can wait for him in the dry?'

That's what I love about the country. Hello, I see you're a total stranger; why don't you come in? You've got at least an hour to clean the place out, if you need that long. Dearie.

'Thanks, that's really thoughtful of you.'

'I'll get the key then, dearie.'

Of course, I realized that I could not betray the trust that Ethelred and the old biddy placed in me. Once I'd gone through all his stuff, I'd have to make sure I put it back *exactly* where it had been before.

Geraldine's accounts were the first thing that came to hand. It was all much as Ethelred had said – a balance of £92.57. The tiny detail that he'd missed was that just over £600,000 had been transferred out of the account just before Geraldine disappeared. But perhaps he had simply forgotten to mention that.

So where had the money gone? It was at this moment that the second stroke of luck occurred. The phone rang. Obviously I answered it.

'Mr Tressider's phone. Elsie Thirkettle speaking.'

'Oh . . . *who* are you exactly?' said a voice with a faint Scottish accent and a tendency to talk in italics. 'I wanted to speak to him about the *estate*.'

'I am Mr Tressider's agent.'

'Agent? Oh, so you're what . . . an *accountant*? Are you working on the estate on his behalf?'

'Yes.' It seemed a more promising answer than 'no' and I had, after all, just been helpfully reading the accounts for him.

'Well, it's Mr Smith, the manager of Mrs Tressider's *bank*. Has Mr Tressider briefed you fully on the bank transfer to *Switzerland*?'

The name was obviously familiar, in the sense that he was the shit who had driven Ethelred out of civilized society. I was tempted to elaborate on this theme there and then, but I reasoned that to do so might delay his telling me whatever he was about to tell me. So I just did my best to sound brisk and on the ball. I could always tell him he was a king arsehole later on.

'Absolutely,' I said. 'Just over six hundred thousand. Yes, that puzzled us a great deal.'

'*Puzzled*? I thought I had explained it to him.'

'Oh, you had. I mean it was the detail that puzzled us.'

'I see . . .' He seemed to doubt my credentials. 'Perhaps after all I had better wait until Mr Tressider is available.'

'Negative, Mr Smith,' I said with what I hoped was effectiveness, efficiency and so on. 'He specifically said that he wished me to take care of this for him. I am an expert in this particular field. It would be much easier if you explained it to me first hand.'

'Are you?' He still sounded doubtful for some reason. Why, oh why, this lack of trust? 'Very well. You understand that my interest in this is limited to the loan of three hundred thousand.'

'Which you would like returned to the bank,' I said, pleased with my deductive logic.

'Really, has Mr Tressider explained *nothing* to you? This was a *personal* loan from me to Mrs Tressider without security, which might seem a little foolish but . . . I'm sorry . . . did you say something?'

'No,' I lied.

'Tell Mr Tressider that I have made one more attempt to find out more from the Swiss bank but that they *refused* to let me have the details. All they would say is that the account to which the money was transferred is *not* in the name of Tressider. Of course, we might have guessed that she would open the account in some other name, under the circumstances.'

'And you want me to . . . ?' I enquired.

'Find out whose name the account is in, and recover the *money*, for God's *sake*.' I could positively hear him shaking his head at the other end, but he had now told me too much *not* to trust me. He gave me the name and phone number of the bank and the account number to which the money had been transferred.

So all I now had to do was phone the Swiss bank and get them to divulge to me what they would not tell Geraldine's own bank manager. Piece of piss, really.

I had to make a preliminary call to a mate of mine at Scotland Yard. Thank goodness there are still some policemen with literary ambitions.

'Bill, it's Elsie, I need a favour.'

'Is it anything like the last one?' he asked.

'Maybe a bit.'

'Then no,' he said. 'Definitely not.'

'An author of mine is having a problem,' I went on. 'One of his characters needs to persuade a Swiss bank that he's from the fraud squad. How would you do that exactly?'

The bank proved to be very cooperative and immediately agreed to let me have the information I wanted as soon as they could. For the record I have to point out that I have absolutely no idea how they got the impression during the course of our conversation that I was from Scotland Yard.

It took them less than ten minutes to get back to me.

'Can I speak to Inspector Elsie Thirkettle, please?'

'Speaking.'

'The account is in the name of Pamela Hamilton-Boswell.'

'Let me just note that.'

'I regret however that we can be of little further assistance to you.'

'Why? I thought that I had made it clear that this was a very serious case of fraud.'

'It isn't that. The account has been closed. Miss Hamilton-Boswell withdrew the money in cash.'

'All of it?'

'Every last centime. Is there any further information that you need?'

I was about to say 'no', when it occurred to me to ask when the money had been withdrawn. I scribbled the date down. It was the day after Geraldine's murder. The day *after* Geraldine's murder. This was a pity because my working hypothesis was, of course, that Geraldine and Pamela were one and the same.

'Are you sure that it was Miss Hamilton-Boswell herself?' I asked.

'No. We always release sums of that sort without proof of identity.' This was interesting in the sense that I hadn't realized that Swiss banks did irony.

'And you're equally sure of the date?'

'Obviously.'

'Can you give me a description of the lady who collected the money?'

There was a chuckle somewhere in Switzerland. 'I am so very sorry. Our computer records do not include a photograph of all our customers. She would obviously have provided the necessary identification at the time. Yes, looking at our records, I have a note to the effect that she produced her passport.'

'Young? Old?'

'I can at least tell you that. Let me see. From her date of birth she would be ... let me see ... thirty-nine. What would you call that – old or young?'

'Exactly my age,' I said.

'Would you like me to confirm this information in writing to you at Scotland Yard?'

'That won't be necessary,' I said perhaps a little too quickly. 'Thank you. You have been most helpful.'

'We are always pleased to be of service to Scotland Yard. By the way, we thought that you were in London, whereas the telephone number you gave us appears to be—'

'Serious Fraud Unit,' I said even more quickly. 'We don't publicize our existence.'

'I see. Good afternoon then, Inspector Thirkettle.'

'*Merci beaucoup,*' I replied.

Well, old-world courtesy and politeness cost nothing, I always say.

Obviously, Hamilton-Boswell was not the most common of names. Directory enquiries do not usually provide telephone numbers unless you know the address too. Still, it was going to be easier than the Swiss bank, I reckoned.

There proved to be only five Hamilton-Boswells in the telephone directory. None were Pamela or even had a P as one of their initials. Four were in Scotland, but I ruled them out in favour of the fifth: a major, who lived in a little village in Essex. It was a village I happened to know quite well. Well, there's a coincidence, I thought.

I rang the number and a man answered – oldish, I guessed from his voice. Pamela's father rather than her husband.

'Is that Major Hamilton-Boswell?' I asked.

'It is.'

'Could I speak to Pamela, please?'

There was a funny pause at the other end of the phone.

'Who are you?' he asked.

'A friend of Pamela's.'

'A friend of Pamela's?' He made it sound as though it was a surprise that Pamela had any friends. A little harsh, I thought.

'Yes,' I pressed on. 'A friend from college.' It seemed a safer bet than a friend from school, since, working on the theory that Pamela was his daughter, the Major might know all of the school friends. And 'college' might mean sixth form college or university or veterinary school or whatever. We would have to see in due course what I meant.

'You knew Pamela at *college*?'

'That's right,' I said with more confidence than I was now feeling.

'Pamela *Hamilton-Boswell*?'

I should have been getting used to people talking to me in strange typefaces, but this last couple of italics threw me. Why the emphasis on the surname? Was it that she was called something else now? Married perhaps? Or what? I needed time to think, but instead there I was plunging ahead, on the slippery slope and about to go completely out of control. 'Oh yes,' I heard myself say. 'Didn't she marry . . . that nice What's-his-name?'

There was a much longer pause, then he said, very very slowly and very very carefully, 'I don't know what sort of a sick joke this is, but you really should be ashamed of yourself.'

I pride myself that a lesser person might at this stage have mumbled something about a wrong number and hung up, but I don't let go easily. 'Has something happened to Pamela?' I asked. 'It's a while since I saw her. I really need to know.'

There was a sort of strangled chuckle at the other end. 'Happened to Pamela? Nothing's happened to Pamela, as you put it, for a very long time. But I promise you this. If you dare phone this number again, I shall have the call traced and reported to the police.'

I was tempted to point out that he was addressing an apprentice herring seller from Scotland Yard, but under the circumstances it seemed better to hang up abruptly and pray that he didn't dial 1471 to check out my (that is to say Ethelred's) number.

As I say, I knew the village where the Hamilton-Boswells were living, and the location was too much of a coincidence to be ... well, a coincidence. There was more to this than met the eye, which was saying a great deal.

I fetched a road atlas from the bookcase and studied it. Feldingham was one of those out-of-the-way villages on the marshy bit of coast that lies to the north of the Thames. I know that God-forsaken part of the world well. A damp little church in a damp little churchyard. A damp little pub full of local teddy boys, washed up on some high tide in the late fifties and left there slowly shrivelling. Picturesque fishing boats rotting on the mud-flats. A picturesque container terminal on the far side of the estuary. And the damp, dark green reek of the marshes. Oh, yes, I'm an Essex Girl born and bred all right. Love the place to bits, though next time round do please remind me to be born in Surrey.

This was undoubtedly a three-bar-of-chocolate problem, so I went in search of some. It took a while to dig a bar out from the back of a cupboard, but it was clear from its position, under a rice packet, that Ethelred had forgotten its existence. You don't leave chocolate in the cupboard under a rice packet if you remember you have it. At least, normal people don't. Chocolate in a cupboard is public property.

I took it back to the sitting room to study the map. Feldingham was perhaps two and a half hours' rapid drive away via the Dartford tunnel. A visit today was on the cards if Ethelred came back soon and we made an immediate start.

All I needed to do was get the various papers back in place and finish the chocolate before he returned. He was due to be away for an hour so that meant he would be back . . . I checked my watch . . . fifteen minutes ago. Shit!

But even as I reached for the bank statements, I heard a key turn in the lock. The front door opened. The last thing I wanted was Ethelred now. But nobody came through the sitting-room door. There was an ominous silence. I was forced to correct my earlier statement. The last thing I wanted was a burglar right now. Ethelred would be fine. Then suddenly Ethelred burst into the room, giving me the fright of my life.

Frankly anybody in green wellies and a Barbour looks a prat in my book. Anyone in green wellies and a Barbour who bursts into their own sitting room with a stick in their hand is a total dickhead.

'What are you playing at, Ethelred, you tart?' I said.

He looked fairly peeved, though I couldn't for the life of me understand why. I looked at the chocolate, then at the general mess around me and then back to the chocolate again.

'Oh, for goodness' sake,' I said. 'It was in the *cupboard*.'

Thirteen

From the moment I saw Elsie sitting joyfully in the midst of so many things that did not belong to her, I knew that matters had taken a turn for the worse. As she described her clumsy attempts at detective work I could only groan inwardly. Particularly excruciating was her account of her conversation with Major Hamilton-Boswell.

'For Christ's sake,' I said. 'Can't you recognize when you're way off track? His daughter – or whoever she is – clearly has nothing to do with the bank account in Switzerland. The poor man must have thought you were crazy.'

'But Ethelred,' said Elsie. 'It's Feldingham. *Feldingham.* Doesn't the name mean anything to you?'

'I don't see what you're getting at,' I said.

'Feldingham, Ethelred. Stop playing the idiot boy for a moment and cast your mind back to an ill-omened day in June, many a year ago. You were wearing a grey morning suit and a top hat, if that helps you at all. You had a carnation in your button hole. There was a bitch hanging off your left arm. I was there in a lemon-coloured frock, which I have since graciously bestowed on the Oxfam shop.'

'All right,' I sighed. 'I got married there. So what?'

'You got married there because Geraldine's parents lived there and had done so for many years. Geraldine grew up there. Her sister still lives there. Come on, Ethelred. Of all the joints in all the world, the only Hamilton-Boswell in England shows up in this one. That is not a coincidence. That is deeply, deeply suspicious. It needs following up.'

'You are not going to visit the Hamilton-Boswells.'

'I agree that that might be inadvisable. But we can visit Geraldine's sister, Miss Charlotte Turner.'

'I am not going off on a wild-goose chase to the depths of Essex.'

'Fine, I'll go on my own, then.'

'You don't know where Charlotte lives.'

'I didn't know where the Hamilton-Boswells lived.'

I sighed again. 'OK, I'll come. But only to stop you making a total fool of yourself.'

'Thought you might,' said Elsie.

God, she can be smug at times.

It was a long drive through low, unambitious countryside. The road wound over gentle rises and falls in the ground that could make up their minds neither to be proper hills nor satisfactory valleys. Occasionally a new vista would slyly suggest that more might be on offer, only to fail to deliver anything that we had not seen before. We passed through tacky, strung-out settlements with no pretensions to be any more than that. Only billboards and breakers' yards added a touch of class to the scene. As we approached the coast, you could taste the salt and decay of the marshlands. The old white weather-board houses and meagre flint churches seemed to crouch and huddle together against a wind that blew across the North Sea straight from the steppes. This was a flat land, merely on loan from the ocean, and prevented only by the snaking dykes and sea walls from returning at the next high tide to the salt water from which it came.

St Peter's church is a modest brick-and-flint building with a stumpy wooden steeple and a large green churchyard full of mossy and largely unreadable gravestones. As Feldingham has grown, piety has declined proportionately; the need has never arisen to enhance what Fairfax would have approved as a perfectly good Norman building.

I succeeded in convincing Elsie that I had no wish to revisit the scene of my wedding and we passed on to the far side of the village where Charlotte's substantial, boxy, modern house lay in well-tended grounds.

I was of course well aware that Charlotte had never liked me, but her dislike had taken the form of a certain aloofness rather than actual antagonism. As with others who had featured, either as major players or in walk-on parts, during my divorce, I had good reason to feel sorry for her now rather than harbour any ill feeling. For her part, Charlotte greeted us with her usual indifference.

Charlotte was some three or four years older than her sister. Old enough certainly to give her a lifelong sense of superiority and to regard Geraldine, rightly, as an irresponsible child forever having to be pulled out of life's muddy puddles. They resembled each other only superficially in appearance and not at all in character. While there was some facial similarity, Charlotte was taller, more solidly built than Geraldine: one of nature's hockey players. She had inherited at birth the mantle of the sensible one. Even in photographs of her as quite a small child there was a seriousness about her: more showed her frowning than smiling and in all there was a firmness in her gaze that suggested that here was a kid who wouldn't stand for any nonsense. But even she must have been briefly susceptible to Geraldine's charms, because she had, after all, also invested a sizeable sum of money in the last failed project. Unlike Rupert or (in a different way) Smith-the-Bank, she could afford to lose the money. She had inherited a house from her parents. She had a good job and no family dependent on her. In this last respect she had always struck me as rather lonely. I don't believe that she had actually been jilted at the altar, but there had, in the distant past, been some disappointments – a broken engagement possibly, an unrequited passion for some rugby-playing merchant banker. Or then again, perhaps not. How was I to tell? She never was the sort of person to share intimate details of that nature with a brother-in-law, unlike Geraldine, who would share anyone's secrets at the drop of a hat with a total stranger. She was also the exact reverse of Geraldine in one other important respect: she was essentially a very unhappy person.

'I've made you tea,' she said. 'I believe that's what one is supposed to do under these circumstances. The grieving family assembles for cucumber sandwiches and a little hypocrisy.'

It was remarkable that she could inject such a note of bitterness into the offer of a cup of tea.

'Thank you,' I said.

'Ta,' said Elsie, on what passed for her best behaviour for the moment. I watched her juggle a cup of tea and a plate ornamented by a single, impossibly thin cucumber sandwich.

Charlotte put down the teapot and placed a tea cosy over it. (I tried to remember when I had last had tea that had not been made with a tea bag in a mug.) 'So, what really brings you here?'

'Oh, a chance to drive out into the country and revisit the happy scene of my wedding day. You're lucky: it's so peaceful round here.'

'Don't you believe it. They broke into the church early this year and did all sorts of damage – they even stole the parish registers, if you'll believe that. So, that's the record of your marriage lost and gone. I know why you've come here. It's the money, isn't it? And I assume that the cash, like everything else, is also lost and gone for ever?' Charlotte was not the sort of person to waste a great deal of time on small talk.

'Probably.'

'Pretty much what I expected. God, what a cow my sister was. I suppose you've been lumbered with clearing up her mess?'

I nodded, thinking as I did so that these were probably the most sympathetic words that Charlotte had ever addressed to me.

'Have you fixed a date for the funeral?' she continued.

I took a sip of my tea. 'I'd like to get on with it, but I don't yet know when they'll release the body.'

'I suppose I'll have to go, but don't expect me to weep over the coffin or anything. I'm not saying that I would have strangled her myself, but I can understand how somebody might decide it was a sound plan. Did the police question you?'

'Yes,' I said.

'Me too,' she said with a certain relish. 'I was here in good old Feldingham, God rot it, on the relevant date – at a meeting of the WI, as it happened. Deadly boring but an impeccable alibi. And no mere police sergeant is going to be able to browbeat the chairwoman of the WI into saying something that she doesn't want to say. Tough job for the police all round. If they need to talk to everyone who wanted Geraldine dead, they'll have to interview half the Home Counties.'

'Not quite. She had her good points too,' I said.

'Sorry,' said Charlotte. 'I keep forgetting that you alone never saw through her. And you had to identify the body. That can't have been much fun.'

'It was all surprisingly matter-of-fact.'

'Still, it can't have been pleasant seeing somebody you were once fond of stretched out cold on a slab like a pound of cod. I assume that's what she looked like? You used to show her a dog-like devotion that I never quite understood, so you have my sympathy now, for what it's worth . . .'

'Does the name Pamela Hamilton-Boswell mean anything to you?' demanded Elsie, apparently finding this polite chit-chat a bit off the point.

Charlotte frowned. 'Yes, definitely,' she said. 'What is this? A trivia quiz?' She tapped her fingers on the table for a moment. 'Didn't she present *Blue Peter* back in the sixties? Something like that. The name is really familiar anyway.'

'She'd be about your age – maybe a bit younger,' said Elsie.

'My age? Wait a minute. I remember now!' Then she chanted in an eery voice, ' "*Pamela Hamilton-Boswell, she's pushing back the stone. Pamela Hamilton-Boswell, she glides the road alone. Pamela Hamilton-Boswell, she's creeping up your stair. Pamela Hamilton-Boswell is there, there, there!*" ' Charlotte laughed. 'It's years since I thought of that. It's a rhyme that Geraldine and I made up to frighten each other. Chanted in the dark at about midnight it can be quite effective.'

'But who *was* she?' demanded Elsie.

'Oh, she was the little girl who died,' said Charlotte. 'You're right. She was roughly Geraldine's age, but she was only . . . oh, just one or two when she died. If we ever met her when she was alive, I don't remember it, though I do think I recall being told at the time about her being ill. Leukaemia, I think it was: they couldn't treat it as well in those days, so I guess it was a death sentence from the moment they diagnosed it. Horrible for the parents. She's buried at St Peter's. We used to walk past her gravestone every Sunday. It was the first hint we had that it wasn't only old people who died: it could happen to children like us as well. The fact that she was almost exactly our age reinforced the message, I suppose. Her parents must still live in the village: Colonel and Mrs Hamilton-Boswell.'

'Major and Mrs,' said Elsie.

'That's right. Major and Mrs. Gosh, you are well informed on our little village. So what has she got to do with anything?'

'Would she have ever had a bank account in Switzerland?' asked Elsie.

Charlotte threw back her head and guffawed. 'What an extraordinary idea!'

'Then somebody opened one in her name.'

'Geraldine, you mean?' said Charlotte, raising an eyebrow.

'Possibly. But if so, she drew the money out the day after she died,' said Elsie.

Charlotte looked at me, then back at Elsie. 'I'm not sure what you are suggesting?'

'An accomplice. Another woman of about the same age, and not totally dissimilar appearance, with access to Geraldine's papers.'

'I hope you are not suggesting that that was me.'

'It could have been.' If I had been prepared to forgive and forget, Elsie clearly was not. She had been waiting for a chance to have a dig at Charlotte, and this appeared to be it.

'I have already accounted to the police for my movements. I don't think I need to account to you as well.'

'You have to admit there wouldn't have been many people in a better position than you to do it.'

Charlotte got to her feet. For a moment I thought that she might be about to pick Elsie up bodily and throw her out. But she merely removed the cosy from the teapot and said: 'But I didn't, did I? Now, more tea anyone?'

'You don't have a bar of Fruit & Nut by any chance?' enquired Elsie. 'Ouch,' she added as I kicked her.

As we passed the church for the second time, on our way out of the village, I could not avoid stopping the car and walking, in the fast-fading light, along the church path to a gravestone not far from the lych-gate.

PAMELA HAMILTON-BOSWELL
Born 12-2-65
Died 13-11-67
May angels guide thee to thy rest

Muttering, 'They'll never miss one,' Elsie took a rose from a large bunch on a nearby grave and propped it against Pamela Hamilton-Boswell's gravestone. 'Poor little sod,' she added. 'Where's the divine purpose in that, eh?'

As we walked back she rubbed her eyes a couple of times and sniffed.

'Must be getting a cold,' she said quickly, before I could enquire further.

We drove home slowly in a mist that had crept in silently and insidiously from the sea, enveloping the dark fields and trees and throwing back the beam from my headlights.

'Well, I think we can rule her out,' Elsie conceded.

'I'm glad you admit that it was all a waste of time,' I said.

'Oh, not a waste of time,' she said. 'Far from it. We know who Pamela Hamilton-Boswell is now, and we can be absolutely certain that it was Geraldine who came up with the name for the account. It confirms that Geraldine's disappearance was long planned: she'd set up a bank account in a false name to transfer funds into. And, since Geraldine could not have withdrawn the money herself, we know that somebody else was sufficiently aware of her plans to withdraw the cash after she died. An accomplice had always seemed likely, but I had assumed that it must be a man. I think we are looking for a woman, who knew Geraldine well and who possibly lives in Essex.' She paused for a moment, then: 'That's it!' she said. 'Stop the car!'

'Stop? Here?' There was no sign, on the narrow lane along which we were driving, of any safe stopping place, above all in this mist. I slowed down, my eyes searching right and left for any piece of verge wide enough to take a medium-sized saloon car.

'Ethelred, you silly tart. What are you doing? You'll kill us stopping here. Clearly when I say stop the car, I am speaking figuratively. What I mean is . . .' Elsie consulted my map, '. . . turn left in about two and a half miles.'

'Can I ask why?'

'Elizabeth.'

'But surely not—'

'We must leave no stone unturned.'

I put my foot on the accelerator too late. In my rear-view mirror I saw headlights approach with horrible rapidity and swerve to the right. A large dark object passed us at speed, sounding its horn in annoyance. I allowed the car to slowly build up speed as we set off again along the lane, watching carefully for a left turning.

Elizabeth's house was in complete contrast to Charlotte's modern, safe, oddly suburban home. A short stretch of gravel drive led us to the front of one of the large half-timbered farmhouses in which that part of Essex abounds. Once the homes of yeoman farmers, they are now usually the country residences of prosperous scrap dealers or upmarket pornographers. I could not remember which, if either, of these professions Elizabeth's second husband, Dennis, followed – though whatever it was made him a great deal of money, as Elizabeth often reminded me. I had met him once or twice because Elizabeth, in the wake of Rupert's desertion, had seen me as some sort of ally. We had offered each other (purely verbal) consolation and I had been invited to her wedding a year or two after the divorce from Rupert. We had exchanged Christmas cards subsequently (hers large and with a customized message printed inside) but I had never visited her new house. Elsie did not explain from where she had obtained Elizabeth's address, though it was quite possibly from a surreptitious reading of my address book.

It was not only Elizabeth's house but her person that presented a contrast with Charlotte. Like Charlotte and Geraldine, Elizabeth was blonde, but there all similarity ended. Delicate and petite, she had sometimes struck me as resembling a small startled deer; albeit a very determined deer who was utterly convinced of the rightness of her cause. Conventionally, she should have been a beauty – slim, blonde, fine-featured – but there was a semi-permanent down-turn of her mouth, which left one with the feeling that she was, in the end, unremarkable. To describe her as plain – something that I think I may have implied before – is perhaps a little unfair, but she did not turn heads in the street. Nor did she have any special talents that I was aware of. Viewing her current opulence, you could only feel that this was a small deer that had landed neatly on its hoofs.

She greeted me warmly but without surprise. The preparations for an indulgently late children's bed-time were handed over to a young but apparently efficient nanny, who whisked a small girl and boy off up a flight of heavily carved oak stairs to what was (I was sure) a warm bathroom full of steam and soft, thick towels.

We in turn were led through into a large, black-beamed sitting room, with low ceilings and a vast inglenook fireplace. Elizabeth added another log to an already more than adequate blaze before saying to me, 'Well, I suppose I don't need to ask what brings you here.'

'I assume that the police contacted you as well?' I asked.

'Of course. I was pleased to discover that I was a prime suspect.'

'Rupert did say that you had issued death threats,' I observed.

Elizabeth gave a funny little laugh. 'Death threats? *Moi*? The poor boy always did have a vivid imagination. I would scarcely have wasted time on Geraldine. Why should I? The silly woman saved me from a lifetime of penury. Rupert was never going to earn any money. He wasn't going to inherit much either.'

'He must have inherited some,' I said. 'Geraldine managed to defraud him of two hundred thousand just before she vanished.'

'Oh, do me a favour,' said Elizabeth, in tones that she had certainly acquired from her second husband. 'That's not *money*. Dennis earns more than that in a year. Much more.'

'He doesn't need an agent, does he?' asked Elsie, who could calculate 12½ per cent of any figure in nanoseconds.

Elizabeth made a nervous, thin-lipped smile, in the way that she did when she did not entirely understand something, which in the old days had been quite often.

'So, did the police give you a hard time?' she asked me.

'Not really. I was in Châteauneuf-sur-Loire at the critical time. You?'

'I was on a business trip with Dennis. Strasbourg.'

Elsie mouthed at me, 'SWITZERLAND?'

I mouthed back: 'FRANCE.' I was going to add, 'Former imperial free city, now seat of the European Parliament,' but it's a tricky one to mouth in full.

'We were there for four days,' Elizabeth continued. 'Apparently we arrived the day before Geraldine vanished. The constabulary lost interest in me pretty quickly anyway. Much to Dennis's relief: the Old Bill make him jittery, he says.'

I bet, I thought. 'They seem to suspect a serial killer,' I said.

Elizabeth shrugged. 'Well, I had nothing to do with it, obviously. Why should I? I would scarcely want to risk all of this for a bit of petty revenge on a stupid cow like Geraldine. The police saw that straight away.'

'And how was Strasbourg?' I asked.

'Oh, dull. Good shopping. Good food. But dull. I only really went to keep an eye on Dennis. Stop watching him for a moment and . . .' She gave a glance at the ceiling above.

'He's screwing the nanny?' asked Elsie with her usual sensitivity and tact.

'Not this one, or at least not yet. But the last one . . . She had to go, obviously. Dennis thought I might leave him.' Elizabeth gave a funny, strangled sort of laugh. 'He should be so lucky. There was never the slightest question about who would be going out through that door. Any more trouble and he knows I'll take the kids, the house and every penny he's got.' Just for a moment a look of such intensity crossed her face that I could have believed her capable of almost anything to protect what she had gained. Then the face relaxed again and she smiled. 'It will be another fifteen minutes until the children want their bed-time story. Would you like a tour of the house? It's listed. Grade Two Star. That's heaps better than Grade Two.'

I offered to drop Elsie off in Hampstead, but that, as she pointed out, left her car stranded in Findon. Since it would be too late, once in Findon, for her to drive back again to London that night, we agreed that one or other of us would have to sleep on the sofa, while Elsie slept in my bed.

For most of the journey Elsie remained deep in thought. We proceeded together over the Dartford Bridge in silence, the river black and silvery far beneath us. The rain started to fall heavily as we drove back through Kent. Once or twice I found myself almost dropping off to sleep, lulled towards an easy slumber by the gentle sound of the windscreen wipers beating out their rhythm and the tyres sloshing through the surface water.

Somewhere near Crawley, Elsie broke her unaccustomed abstinence from speech. 'Ethelred,' she said suddenly. 'If you did bump Geraldine off, then, however you managed it and whenever it was you did it, I'll say you were with me in Hampstead. I'll say you were in bed with me, if it would help.'

It was too dark for her to see my smile. 'That really won't be necessary,' I said. 'I was in France and not in bed with anyone.'

'Just so long as you know the offer is there. For that evening or any other.'

'Thank you. But I won't need it.'

We drove up to Greypoint House a little after eleven thirty with the rain still falling. I was surprised to see a police car outside. As I parked the car a uniformed officer and a detective got out and walked over towards me.

'Good evening, Mr Tressider. We would be grateful if you would accompany us to the police station to answer some further questions.'

'I suppose it can't wait until tomorrow morning?' I asked.

'I am afraid not,' said the detective.

'I am obviously keen to help you but I really am very tired.'

'This is not an optional visit,' said the detective.

'Am I under arrest?' I asked.

'Not at present, but that could be arranged.'

'You don't seem to be offering me much choice.'

'That's right,' said the detective with a smile. 'Shall we go?'

I was driven into Worthing in the police car, leaving Elsie to make herself at home in my flat. It was the fastest journey into town I have ever done, though to my disappointment they did not switch the siren on, thus depriving me of an ambition I have had since boyhood.

As we entered one of the small, stuffy interview rooms at the police station, my tiredness was replaced with a cautious alertness. I still did not sense danger exactly, but I knew that I would need to be careful over the next hour – perhaps over the next two or three hours. There were still questions that I was keen not to have to answer and, in any case, it would be useful to know how much, if anything, they knew that I did not.

The detective returned with an inspector, who switched on a small tape-recording device and announced to it who was present in the room and that it was by now somewhat after midnight.

'We think, Ethelred, that you may be able to help us a little further with our inquiries.'

'Mr Tressider,' I said. 'You call me Mr Tressider. I call you Inspector, unless you have some other form of address you prefer.'

He was slightly taken aback by this. 'Very well – Mr Tressider – have you seen this before?' He turned to the recording machine and addressed it: 'I am showing *Mr* Tressider exhibit A.'

He handed me, in a clear plastic case, Geraldine's 'suicide' note. I looked at it briefly.

'I have seen a photocopy before. I've never seen the original,' I said, handing it back to him.

The inspector and detective exchanged a significant glance.

'Can we get this straight,' said the inspector slowly. 'You have never seen the original of the suicide note before?'

'Never in my life.'

'Then perhaps you could explain – *Mr* Tressider – why it has your fingerprints all over it?'

Fourteen

It was a bit like those poxy Rubik's cubes that everyone used to buy – bloody stupid things. Basically you start with a cube that's all red on one side, all blue on another, all green on the third, and so on and so on. Then you twist them round so that the colours are all mixed up. Then you twist them round again to get them back where you started. Now, you will immediately see two objections to this. 1) If you want them back as they were, why mess with them in the first place? And 2) nobody I know has *ever* managed to get them back the way they were without a large hammer and a tube of glue. You get one side all red and another all yellow, then you twist it around to get a third all orange and you've mucked up the other two. Then you get the yellow one right, and you've lost the sodding orange one. There was a time when you found a lot of them in Oxfam shops.

It was like that with Geraldine's murder, but without the Oxfam get-out. As soon as I got one bit of the story clear in my head, I realized that it had just put another bit out of joint. So, as we splashed our way southwards that evening, through dark and wet Essex and darker, wetter Kent, I kept turning the problem this way and that.

Geraldine was dead. When it came down to it, I decided, that was the only stone-cold certainty. And of course she had been planning to disappear. (Probably.) The 'suicide' fitted neatly into a disappearing scheme. So did opening a bank account in an assumed name and transferring large sums of money that didn't belong to her out the country.

Then there were plenty of things pointing to an accomplice. How had she hoped to get away from West Wittering – particularly dressed as she had been? What were the funny yellow dots in her flat that Ethelred had been so keen to write off as red herrings? Were they to help somebody who was going to organize things for her after she left? Yes, definitely. But who? And why hadn't that person shown up to do whatever it was he or she was supposed to do?

Something had clearly gone badly wrong with the plan, because, before Geraldine could fly off to Switzerland as planned, somebody strangled her and left her body on Cissbury Ring. Then somebody went and cleaned out the bank account in Switzerland. So was the person who killed her the same one who went to Switzerland?

Then there was something else that kept coming back to me: Why West Wittering? Why Cissbury Ring? I mean, there's lots of coastline. It's all over the place: sand, salty water, seagull crap. There's really no shortage of the stuff. For Christ's sake, why Sussex? It all seemed deliberately designed to throw suspicion on Ethelred. But Ethelred would scarcely have chosen Cissbury Ring to dump a body, so if somebody was trying to pin the murder on him, it wasn't even subtle. And he was in *France*.

Wasn't he?

But equally I didn't buy the police theory, as explained to me by Ethelred, that Geraldine had, quite coincidentally, been murdered by a serial killer. The other victims had been Sad Cows, whereas Geraldine was a Scheming Bitch – another species entirely. Your experienced serial killer would scarcely be so careless as to murder one in mistake for the other. Geraldine was not the sort of person to fall into the crude type of trap that had been laid for the other victims. And how did the police theory explain – assuming they knew about it – the withdrawal of the cash?

And deep down I was certain that Ethelred knew a great deal more than he was telling me. He hadn't the slightest interest in finding Geraldine's killer. In spite of everything he said, he really had no interest in finding the money either. But there was something else that he was *desperate* to know, and he had no intention of telling me what it was. Yes, Ethelred was about to make a total idiot of himself. On second thoughts, in the end, *that* was the thing I was most certain of.

We must have been well past the Dartford Bridge when I turned to Ethelred and said: 'If you did bump Geraldine off, then, however you managed it and whenever it was you did it, I'll say you were with me in Hampstead. I'll say you were in bed with me, if it would help.'

'That really won't be necessary,' he said. 'I was in France and not in bed with anyone.'

'Just so long as you know the offer is there. For that evening or any other,' I said. I was shocked to realize that by 'any other' I meant future evenings as well as past.

'Thank you. But I won't need it,' he said.

At that moment his face was lit up by the headlights of an oncoming car. I saw him clearly only for a second or so, but he had a broad grin on his face. He really was quite pleased with himself. You silly tart, I thought, what *are* you playing at?

It was no surprise to *me* when the police took him away.

Once inside the flat, however, my mind started working fast. The more information I had, the easier it would be to help Ethelred. What he wouldn't tell me, I had to find out for myself. The last time I was in his flat I'd had an hour or so to find what I wanted. This time I reckoned I had thirty years, less time off for good behaviour. Still, there was no harm in making a start.

The first thing to decide was who might have information that I didn't. A quick flick through Ethelred's address book turned up the Office Boy, Darren Oxtoby. On the journey to Feldingham I had wheedled a little bit of information out of Ethelred about young Darren. I knew that he had worked for Geraldine for a while and that he was a writer (or at least wanted to be a writer), which might work to my advantage. It was a bit after midnight, so what would a keen young writer be doing? Burning the old midnight oil and working on his masterpiece, obviously. So it wasn't too late to call him.

The phone rang for a bit and then a slightly confused voice answered.

'Yes?'

'Sorry, Darren, did I disturb your writing?'

'I was asleep. Who is that?'

So that's writing a masterpiece or sleeping – obviously. Still, I'd got his attention, which was all I needed.

'I'm Elsie Thirkettle. I'm a literary agent.'

'The agent Mr Tressider knows? Are you phoning about the novel?'

Even in his current befuddled state he could not quite believe that respectable agents phoned out of the blue in the middle of the night to talk literature. In a moment he would be fully awake, so I needed to work fast if I was to pump him for information.

'Yes, Darren. Mr Tressider has told me a great deal. But first I need you to answer some simple questions.'

'Questions? Sure. Well, I've been writing for about two years. I had a short story published in *Granta* last year and—'

'No, Darren, not those questions. Different questions, like when did you start working for the Bitch?'

'Mrs Tressider, you mean? About four months ago.'

'OK. Now think, Darren: Who might have had a motive for killing her? Who really hated her guts?'

'Nobody that I know of. Lots of people phoned the office who were very upset.'

'In what way?'

'Well, she owed them money. Builders. Office supplies. The people who owned the office building. The newsagents. Everyone, really. I had to tell them that their bills were being processed and that they would be paid soon. If they came to the office I had to tell them Mrs Tressider was out.'

'Newsagents don't often murder their customers. Who else was there?'

'There were the shareholders in the company too – like Miss Turner.'

'Geraldine's sister?'

'That's right. There were four or five of them. They kept phoning up. They wanted their money back. But I don't think there was any money.'

'But they all stood less chance of getting their money with Geraldine dead than with her alive. Keep going. Who else?'

'Nobody much. Mrs Tressider was working on a new project – houses in the East End.'

'Was this a serious project?'

'Yes, she used to have meetings with Dennis Rainbird about it.

They met up quite often. For a while I wondered if there wasn't something going on between them.'

Dennis Rainbird? It was a bit like Charlotte when confronted with Pamela Hamilton-Boswell. I knew I knew the name, but who on earth was it? Ah, yes, of course: Elizabeth's husband. That was who Dennis Rainbird was.

There was a stunned silence at my end of the phone, then I said, '*Elizabeth's husband*?'

Newtonian physics dictates that when there is a stunned silence at one end of the phone there will be an equal and opposite stunned silence at the other end of the phone, a silence terminated in this case by Darren saying, 'You what?'

'Dennis Rainbird. I know him,' I said. 'Sort of. Was this just a business relationship or was there more to it than that?'

'I think they were quite good friends.'

'I bet,' I said.

'But you know him, too?'

'That's right.'

'Small world,' observed Darren, with that writer's ability to get straight to the heart of the matter.

'Do you have Dennis Rainbird's work address or telephone number?' I demanded.

'No, but it would be at the office. I can't get in any more. Mr Tressider took my key.'

'Never mind, I should be able to manage that. Thank you, Darren, you have been most helpful. I'll let you get back to sleep now.'

'But my novel ... ?' A note of concern was creeping into his voice. Had he just been stitched up? Well, yes, of course.

'Send me the synopsis and the first two chapters. And don't

forget to enclose the return postage.' I gave him my address, but not my telephone number.

'Is that it?'

'Yep.'

'Goodnight.'

'Goodnight, Darren.'

I could have phoned Elizabeth's number to try to get Dennis at home, but it was now half past midnight and I expected that I would not get the most friendly of receptions, even when I pointed out that I was in a position to blackmail him. (Probably.)

I got out a book of maps – Europe this time. Strasbourg turned out to be up in the top right-hand corner of France and not a million miles away from Switzerland. Which was sort of interesting.

I decided to get some kip. After all, tomorrow could be a long day, depending on whether I headed for Switzerland next or back to Essex. I wouldn't want you to get the impression that I wasn't worried about Ethelred or anything, because I was, but I've never had any trouble in getting off to sleep. It's having a clear conscience, I guess.

I don't know what time I woke up but it was still dark. I was just thinking how odd it was that I had woken up at all, when I realized that I had been disturbed by the noise of somebody moving around in the flat. It took me a few seconds to work out where I was, which meant that I didn't have time to worry about burglars before Ethelred's long, pale face appeared round the door. He grinned at me.

'How did you break out of jail?' I asked.

'No problem,' he said.

'What did the police want anyway?'

He paused for a moment, then said, 'It was nothing much. They found my fingerprints on the suicide note. They just wanted to know how they got there.'

'So how the hell *did* they get there?' I demanded.

Fifteen

'Because it is my writing paper,' I said.

This was not one of the answers that they were expecting.

'*Your* paper?' asked the inspector. As the senior officer present he generally got the best lines. Except that, for the next few minutes, I knew all the best lines were going to be mine.

'Certainly.' I picked up the plastic folder and turned it round so that they could read it more clearly. 'All that is left of the address is N1, which might have led you to think that it was an Islington address and therefore Geraldine's paper. If you were to compare this with a sheet of my wife's writing paper, you would however see that the characters did not match up with the postcode there. That is because the complete postcode on this sheet was BN14 0TF. If you check, you will quickly discover that this is my postcode here in Sussex. And if you look very closely at the sheet of paper, you will notice that you can still see a small bit of the B just before the N.'

They looked. They saw. There was a small bit of a B.

'But you said that you hadn't seen the paper before,' said the sergeant.

'No, I said that I had not seen the suicide note. When I last saw this sheet of paper, it would have been blank, and indeed would have had the address intact.'

'But how,' said the inspector, screwing up his eyes and squinting at me, 'did Mrs Tressider get hold of your paper, if that's what you're telling us? You said that you hadn't seen her for years.'

'Again, I fear that I must correct you. I said that I had not seen my wife for some time. Four or five weeks, I would think. Well, before I went to France, anyway.'

'But I thought—'

'—that I had not seen Geraldine since our divorce? It is true that for some years after we split up we did not see each other at all. It must have been seven or eight months ago, however, that she turned up quite unannounced at my door. She said that she was passing through and thought that she would look me up. She felt that, after all that time, there was no reason why we should not be friends. We had lunch together. Afterwards she wanted my telephone number. I gave her a sheet of my writing paper – doubtless the one you have there – which had both my full postal address and my phone. I have no doubt that she tore off the bit she needed albeit rather carelessly, losing an N1 in the process but with the phone number intact, and then just put the rest aside as scrap paper.'

'Which she later used for a suicide note?'

'So it would seem. She probably didn't even remember where she got it.'

'You think it was a coincidence?'

No, I thought.

'Yes,' I said. 'Pure coincidence, Inspector. If I were going to fake somebody else's suicide note, why would I do it on my own headed paper? I'm a writer, for God's sake. My flat is full of virtually untraceable plain white A4. I'd have used that, wouldn't I? And I would have left no fingerprints. I am a crime writer, after all.'

'So, let's get this straight. You saw your wife quite often in the year leading up to her death?'

'Not that often. Say a dozen times. But I'm not denying we were friends. It was what Geraldine wanted and I have always found it easier in the long run to go along with whatever Geraldine had in mind.'

'Mr Tressider, I have already warned you that withholding evidence is a serious offence.'

'I understand that, Inspector, but I have answered all of your questions truthfully. Whether I last saw my wife a couple of weeks or a couple of years ago is scarcely a matter of any significance to you. The fact is that I was in France at the time of the murder. Nor, I can assure you, will you be able to come up with a motive for my murdering my wife, try as hard as you wish. If I have withheld anything, then I have merely withheld the fact that I was on excellent terms with Geraldine almost up to the day she disappeared.'

The two policemen looked at each other. The inspector coughed. 'Somebody else had handled the paper as well as you, but none of the prints were good enough to enable us to identify them. If these later fingerprints were your wife's – and our guess is that they are – then that would largely support your story.'

'There you are then,' I said.

The inspector turned abruptly to the recording machine and said very distinctly, 'Interview terminated at twelve thirty-seven.' He pressed a button and the whirring noise stopped. I smiled at him. He did not return the smile. The sergeant unplugged the machine without looking at either of us.

'One other thing that you may like to know: Your wife's car has shown up,' said the inspector. 'She sold it – cash obviously – for a suspiciously low price to a punter who now finds himself in possession of a car that a finance company also believes that it owns. Had your wife lived, we would have had a number of questions for her.'

'I don't think that she was planning to hang around to provide answers,' I said.

'Nor do we. Her passport, driving licence and credit cards are still missing. So is the luggage that she would have had with her. Our serial killer did not leave any identification on other bodies, however. It's something else that ties your wife's murder in with the others. That, and the fact that she was blonde and attractive and happened to be in West Sussex.'

'So, it's back to the idea that it was a serial killer?'

'It always would have been if you had simply told us the truth.'

'I did.'

'Not the whole truth.'

'Can I go now?' I asked.

'Is there anything else that you should be telling us, Mr Tressider?' asked the inspector.

'Such as?' I asked. 'Ask away. I am a mine of useful information on the social history of the late fourteenth century. I also know a reasonable amount about the practice of oral and maxillofacial surgery and medieval church architecture.'

The inspector rubbed his eyes. It was turning into a long night for him as well. 'Do you know anything further concerning the murder that we are investigating?' He spoke slowly and menacingly, but he was beaten.

'I promise that I have told you everything I know about that.'

'I hope so,' said the inspector. 'I do so very much hope so.'

My suggestion that a squad car might drive me home rapidly and with the lights flashing was politely declined and I was obliged to walk to the railway station and try to pick up a cab there. I was back in Findon before two, which was not bad going. It could have been worse. Much worse.

It seemed best to give Elsie a reasonably truthful account of the night's work. She had a way of ferreting out things, and minor discrepancies always caused her to jump to conclusions. She would not approve of my having seen Geraldine, but that was scarcely her business. She took it quite well, however, and I was obliged to suffer intensive verbal abuse for no more than ten minutes or so.

The she dropped her own little bombshell.

'Dennis Rainbird?' I asked.

'I wondered if you already knew,' she said, very pleased with herself. 'Clearly not.'

'Why should I know something like that?' I asked.

Elsie shrugged and gave me a funny look.

'OK,' I said. 'OK. I didn't tell you I had seen Geraldine, but that really wasn't relevant to anything.'

She gave me another funny look, but funny looks only get you so far. I'd told her all I was telling her.

'Dennis the Menace. Another prime suspect,' said Elsie.

'Really? Who else is on your list?'

'Smith.'

'Scarcely a killer,' I said, 'though I must admit that I really cannot think what induced him to part with his money and hand it over to Geraldine.'

'Oh, come on,' said Elsie. 'She was shagging him, obviously.'

Elsie can sometimes be a little wide of the mark. 'Smith?' I said. 'Oh, I would scarcely think so. Not really her type.'

'Ethelred. Can we have a reality check here? I don't mean to speak ill of the dead, but your ex-wife slept with anything in trousers. She was the sort of woman that your mother warned you about. All right?'

'You never really knew her,' I said.

'So you've told me before.'

'It's true,' I said.

Elsie gave me one of her pitying looks but she was wasting her time, because I really did know Geraldine better than she did.

'When are we going to see Dirty Den?' she asked after a bit.

'As soon as I can arrange it,' I said. 'Dennis is not somebody you just drop in on. I'll phone his secretary and make an appointment.'

'Don't we lose the element of surprise?'

'Yes,' I said, 'but we aren't going to need it. Even if we did need it, Elizabeth will have already told him that we have been round asking questions.'

'So, what's next?'

'I'm a writer. I'm going to get some sleep, then I rather thought I should get on with some writing.'

'Fairfax?'

'Fairfax.'

'That's OK then,' said Elsie.

Sixteen

In the summer of that year Fairfax worked in an office that looked across the river and the water meadows to the tree-capped hills beyond. The water in the river was brown and sluggish and there were cracks in the mud on each side where the level of the river had fallen. Cattle came down to the water to drink and churned up the mud with their hoofs, but the meadows were dry and the grass was scorched and dusty where the cattle passed on their way to the river.

Between the police station and the river was a road, and lorries went by and the dust that they raised powdered the leaves of the bushes. At night you could listen and hear the lorries rumble under the window and watch the way their headlamps lit up the bushes and shone off the dust on the leaves. The branches rose and fell as the lorries passed, and sometimes a warm breeze blew though Fairfax's open window. But the breeze was cool only in the very early morning, when the grey-blue hills were just visible again and the river was a thin milky line across the dark meadows.

That summer Fairfax knew for the first time that he was old, a thing that is not a matter of having lived a certain number of years, but rather of having only a certain number of years still to live, and also a matter of knowing that there were people you had loved that you would never see again and that there were things that you had done that you would not do again.

Constable Rinaldi knocked respectfully on the door.

'Coffee, Brigadiere?' he asked.

'I would rather have grappa,' said Fairfax.

'There is no grappa,' said Rinaldi apologetically. 'Only this coffee that I have made for you.'

'I have grappa,' said Fairfax. He opened a desk drawer and took out a bottle and two glasses.

'I cannot drink grappa while on duty,' said Rinaldi. 'It is not permitted.'

'It is permitted,' said Fairfax. 'I permit it.'

He poured two glasses and they touched them, first fingers extended. The grappa was very strong and very good.

'Another?' asked Fairfax.

'I cannot drink another,' said Rinaldi. 'I have weakness of the head.'

'Drink another,' said Fairfax. 'Your head will stand it.'

'I cannot,' said Rinaldi. 'You should drink coffee, Brigadiere. Then your head will be clear.'

'Clear for what?'

'I do not know, Brigadiere,' said Rinaldi.

'You ask me not to drink grappa and do not know why you ask. I will tell you. There is nothing for my head to be clear for. Nothing. I am tired, Rinaldi. I am tired and I am old. There is nothing left for me here. Do you believe in God, Rinaldi?'

'No, Brigadiere. I am an atheist. I do not believe in God and I do not trust the priests.'

'I do not trust the priests either, but I do believe in God.'

'What has God got to do with drinking grappa?'

'I do not know, Rinaldi. Perhaps nothing to do with drinking grappa, but something to do with feeling old. I do not know.' Fairfax made as if to put the bottle away in the drawer, but placed it carefully down again on the desk. There were two, perhaps three, fingers of spirit remaining in it.

'You are tired, Brigadiere, just tired. You confuse God and grappa. They are not the same. I too believe in grappa. You should go home and get some rest. You should go home and leave that bottle here.'

'There is another bottle at home, Rinaldi. I have discovered this thing. There is always another bottle somewhere. Sometimes it is grappa. Sometimes it is strega. But there is always another bottle if you wish strongly enough to find it. With God it is a little different, but that is how it is with bottles.'

'I do not understand you, Brigadiere. You should go home and get some rest. It is not good that you are here *all day and all night. A man should go home to his family now and then. It is right.'*

'I have no family, Rinaldi.'

'I am sorry, Brigadiere.'

'Don't worry, Rinaldi. It is not your fault.'

'I will not worry about your not having a family, but I will worry about the grappa. Promise me that you will put the bottle away and go home.'

'I promise, Rinaldi. I promise about the bottle and I promise about home. Just leave me now and I will go home.'

'You will go home?'

'I promise. Scout's honour.'

'Shall I leave the coffee?'

'No, take the coffee. I'll be all right now.'

When Fairfax was absolutely sure that Rinaldi was not coming back, he uncorked the bottle and with a steady hand poured himself another large shot of grappa. After that, there was perhaps one more glassful left in the bottle. Then he would go home, he thought. Then he would go home.

So, it was happening again. Who on earth was this Constable Rinaldi? What was this business with the grappa, which Fairfax had never touched previously, as far as I knew? He drank beer and the more than occasional whisky. But not since the first novel had he actually taken drink into the office. What was Fairfax trying to tell me?

I rolled the mouse and clicked on 'Edit', then on 'Select All', and then I pressed 'Delete'. The chapter vanished from my screen and a blank white page replaced it. I put on my Barbour and boots and set off in the rain up towards Cissbury Ring.

Seventeen

It would be unfair to suggest that my father was nothing more than a failed academic. Though he was able to devote less time to it, his failure in the field of politics was every bit as complete and infinitely more humiliating both for him and for his family.

My father's main defect as a politician was that his views corresponded to those of no known political party. They centred on the idea of a semi-hereditary elected monarchy under which kings (there would be no necessity for queens regnant) would be chosen from amongst the bona fide descendants of King Cerdic of Wessex. The electors would consist of a Witan of wise men, of which my father, for some reason, saw himself as a leading member. Though the proposal was, on the face of it, neither more nor less ridiculous than primogeniture, my father experienced some difficulty in persuading the established political parties that the inclusion of an elected monarchy in their manifestos would sway any floating voters. This puzzled him, but he persevered to the extent of joining the local Conservative party and adopting all of their principles unquestioningly, other than loyalty to the House of Windsor.

My father's progress within the party hierarchy was, to say the least, limited. His suggestions that he might be a suitable parliamentary candidate were met, in some circles, with embarrassed silence. Others assumed that he was making a little joke at his own expense, and reacted with guffaws and hearty slaps on the back. Neither response prevented him from continuing to press his claims. He was eventually allowed to stand as Conservative candidate in a local government election. The ward in question consisted of a large council estate on the edge of town with an outlying cluster of farms and country houses. In later years the residents of council estates were to flock to Margaret Thatcher, just as the middle classes were to rally to Tony Blair. My father however found himself largely ignored on the council estate and smugly patronized in the country houses. In neither location did he find the remotest interest in King Cerdic of Wessex or the creation of a Witan. He set himself the target, which I think he achieved, of personally visiting every house in the ward so that nobody might be unsure what he stood for. The margin of his defeat was the largest ever recorded in any ward in any election in that borough.

In theory my father's political career could only go up from this point, but in fact it continued to bob along at much the same level. He was occasionally entrusted with making a vote of thanks to a visiting speaker or organizing a summer fête. He regularly stood outside polling stations, the rain trickling down the neck of his gabardine, taking the names of voters. He was permitted to do nothing that might offer a platform for advancing his Cerdician vision of a reformed monarchy. He occasionally wrote letters to *The Times* on the subject, for each of which he received a polite but regretful acknowledgement from the editor.

Towards the end of his life my father briefly became a failed theologian. He did not, as one might have expected, press for a revival of the worship of Thor and Woden, nor did he settle on the cult of one or other of the more obscure Saxon saints. It was in fact the Holy Ghost that my father decided to favour with his attentions – a much neglected member of the Trinity, as he pointed out to anyone who would listen.

My father had learned sufficiently from his experiences in the Conservative party not to attempt a root-and-branch reform of the Church of England. He limited himself to giving particular emphasis to any references to the Holy Ghost in the Prayer Book or in the selected hymns. Only on days when the church was almost empty was this peculiarity noticed. It was never commented on by anyone. My mother might have selected relevant hymns and readings for my father's funeral, but, for whatever reasons, chose conventional ones that failed to mention the Holy Ghost at all. If the Holy Ghost was present at the service, it was not immediately apparent. The chairman of the local Conservative party also sent his apologies.

It was only after the funeral that the realization came upon me that I had loved my father. But that is perhaps too common a phenomenon to be worth dwelling on here.

The phone rang. Inevitably it was Elsie.

'When are we going to see Dennis the Menace then?'

'He's out of the country. His secretary says he'll get back to me next week.'

'You're useless. I give you one thing to do and you foul it up. I bet he's around. We should have just gone there.'

'Well, we didn't. And don't try it.'

'How's the book going?'

'Serious concern or polite interest?'

'Eighty-seven and a half per cent polite interest. Twelve and a half per cent serious concern.'

'Badly.'

'Writer's block?'

'Writer's diarrhoea. It flows well, but it's crap. I think that Fairfax is making a bid to be literature.'

'A mistake.'

'I think he's telling me that I either make him literature or he's going to quit. Something like that anyway. He no longer seems to approve of me.'

'Ethelred, you have left your brain in neutral again. *You* write the Fairfax novels. Fairfax is just a figment of your imagination. He has no views other than the views you give him. You can make him do anything you want.'

'Maybe I'm trying to tell myself something then. Anyway, why shouldn't I write the occasional literary novel? I've never quite given up hope of winning the Booker Prize, you know.'

'Ethelred, you are so like your father.'

'I don't see how you can say that. You never met my father.'

'All men grow to be like their fathers. It's the biggest single problem women have.'

Eighteen

Gentle sunshine pierced the haze that enveloped Buckford. It strolled past Buckford Cathedral, pausing only to gild the more repulsive of the two gargoyles with its honeyed rays, then turned sharp left down Market Street. It passed through Mucklegate and, following the one-way system, arrived in front of that dread and august building, Buckford Police HQ. A weaker, less determined ray of sunshine might have left it at that and legged it along the bypass to the Rose and Crown, but this one was made of sterner stuff. Entering through a first-floor window it alighted on the desk of one Sergeant Fairfax, who, up to that point, had been staring pensively out of the window.

The view that had been manfully meeting his gaze was a tranquil one of water meadows, contented cows and blue distant hills. It was a view that seemed to say that the lark was on the wing, the snail was in all likelihood on the thorn and that all was right with the world. Sergeant Fairfax was willing to take the lark and snail intelligence on trust, but begged to differ about the world.

Something gnawed at his heart, and a man with a well-gnawed heart has difficulty in taking a balanced view of life in general.

As if fate had capriciously chosen to demonstrate that things could still get worse, at that moment he heard the footsteps of his superior officer advancing down the corridor. The footsteps paused for a moment just short of Fairfax's door, suggesting that their owner had temporarily forgotten the reason why he had wandered into this relatively remote part of his empire. This was probably the case, because there was a hesitant shuffle before the door finally swung open and Chief Superintendent Emsworth drifted amiably into the room.

Emsworth was dressed in a pair of trousers that a charity shop would have been embarrassed to display, if charity shops had been permitted to sell items of discarded police uniform. His jacket was buttoned in a haphazard fashion that indicated that his mind had been elsewhere, possibly some miles from Buckford, when he fastened it. There still had to be some doubt as to which part of police headquarters his mind was currently in.

'Not disturbing you, am I, Fairfax?' he enquired, quickly adding, 'Quite. Quite. Capital, capital.' He sat down opposite Fairfax and began absent-mindedly taking out the pens that Fairfax kept in a pot on his desk and replacing them one by one.

'Can I help you, sir?'

Emsworth ceased his pen-arranging for a moment and looked thoughtful. 'Yes, there was something. Deuced if I can remember what, though. Have you ever done that,

Fairfax – gone into a room and then forgotten why you had gone there?'

'No, sir.'

'Happens to me all the time.' Emsworth hummed for a bit, and seemed likely to turn his attention to paper clips. 'I suppose it doesn't happen to you because you've got a razor-sharp mind, eat plenty of fish and have been a teetotaller from birth.' Suddenly the light began to dawn on Emsworth's kindly face. 'Of course, that's what I came to talk to you about! Booze!'

'Sir?'

'I understand that you've been hitting the old sauce a bit, Fairfax. Can't reveal the name of my informant. Wouldn't want to get Constable Rinaldi into trouble, eh, what?' Emsworth tapped the side of his nose sagaciously. 'Got nothing against the occasional drink of course. Nothing wrong with a chap getting blotto now and then. My brother Gally was blotto for the greater part of his youth and he's as fit a fifty-seven-year-old as you're likely to meet. But my sources are worried that you are over-doing it, even by Gally's exacting standards.'

Fairfax drew himself up to his full height, a useful pre-liminary whether it is a falsehood or a truth one is about to deny. 'Do you have any complaints about my work, sir?'

'Work? Work?' asked Emsworth as if considering a novel idea. 'My dear fellow, certainly not. I was most impressed by the way you pulled in Ginger McVitie.'

'Perhaps it's as well you dropped by. I'm thinking of quitting anyway,' said Fairfax.

'Quitting the demon drink? Excellent, my dear fellow.'

'Quitting the Police Force. I'm getting too old.'

'Surely not? How old are you?'

'Fifty-eight and a half.'

'There you are then. Gally's only a year younger and has no intention of giving up. Of course, he's never actu- ally done *anything*,' Emsworth conceded, 'so it would not be entirely clear what it was that he was giving up. Look, Fairfax, you're sure that it's not just the weather? The weather does affect people oddly. I had a gardener once who gave his notice every time a thunderstorm was on its way. Regular as clockwork – we thought of lending him to the Met Office.'

'It's not the weather, sir.'

Emsworth racked his brain for other possible causes of distress. In his experience the usual front runners were parental objections to one's plans for marrying a chorus girl (33–1), the threat of the theft of a prize pig (10–1) or an impending interview with his sister Connie (2–1 on). None of these was, on the face of it, likely to apply to Fairfax.

'Perhaps I'm not making much sense, sir,' said Fair- fax.

'Not much, but don't worry, my dear fellow. Perfectly normal. Connie often says the same thing about me.'

'You see, sir—'

The conversation was interrupted by a polite knock on the door and a gentle cough.

'What is it, Beach?' asked Emsworth irritably. 'One of

my sisters on the phone again? Well, you can jolly well tell them I'm busy.'

Constable Beach coughed again apologetically. 'Chief Superintendent Parsloe-Parsloe from Matchingham has been waiting in your office for the past ten minutes.'

'Why on earth should he do a thing like that? Doesn't he have an office of his own in Matchingham?'

'He says he has an appointment to see you, sir. Something, I believe, about a stolen manuscript that will embarrass half Shropshire if its contents are ever revealed to the public.'

'Ah,' said Emsworth, the light dawning. 'An appointment, you say. Very well. We'll have to continue our chat about your chorus-girl trouble some other time, Fairfax. But my advice is to put her into a two-seater and drive rapidly in the direction of Gretna Green. Now, lead on, Beach. Let us have Parsloe-Parsloe, and let there be tea.'

The footsteps receded down the corridor and Fairfax was left to his contemplation of the Buckfordshire countryside. The sun had given up Buckford as a bad job and was taking a short breather behind a cloud. The meadows now looked dull and listless. Somewhere out there a cow with a secret sorrow lowed plaintively.

So what, I asked myself, was that all about? Emsworth? Beach? The Hon. Galahad Threepwood? (Did I say Threepwood? Oh yes, I didn't need to be told who this cast of characters belonged to.) Of course, Elsie was right: I had written it, not Fairfax. But what did it all *mean*? What had happened to the crime that was supposed to be a parallel storyline? And what *was* the unexplained problem that Fairfax was wrestling with? How come Fairfax knew and I still didn't? There was only one thing to be done.

Edit.

Select All.

Delete.

I went to make myself a cup of coffee.

Nineteen

I must have met Dennis Rainbird for the first time shortly before his wedding to Elizabeth. Elizabeth had told me a little about him beforehand and I suppose that I was expecting some sort of cross between an old-world spiv and a nightclub bouncer: a pony-tail probably, a jacket slightly too long, a gold chain almost certainly and a scar or two gained in the line of duty.

He had none of these things. To begin with he proved to be a good ten years older than I, and looked just like the large, prosperous, middle-aged businessman that, in a sense, he actually was. His suits, he explained to me very early in our acquaintance, invariably came from Gieves & Hawkes, his shirts were from Turnbull & Asser, and his brogues were Church's. His aftershave (perhaps a little too much in evidence) was some obscure, but eminently respectable, English brand. His hair was neither too short nor too long and at the sides it was flicked back into two little wings in the accepted upper-middle-class manner. He had an Oxford accent in a way that I (who had actually been to Oxford University) did not. He had a habit of opening doors for ladies that my generation had either forgotten or that our mothers had never taught us. Indeed, he gave the impression that, at some point in his life, he had been stuck on a slow train with nothing but a book on old-world courtesy and had consequently memorized it down to the last semicolon. Perhaps the key to picturing Dennis was to understand that he could dress and behave in this impeccable manner without disguising for a moment that he was basically just a jumped-up East End villain.

A further key may be this: While he was always perfectly happy to tell me what he had paid for his tie or which minor celebrity he had dined with the week before, I never learned anything about where he had come from, who his family were or what he had done with his life prior to the age of, say, thirty-five. I am not suggesting that there were dark secrets, but you were left with the feeling that there might be relatively little to boast of. And if Dennis could not boast of a thing, then it tended to get left out of the conversation altogether.

Dennis's office proved to be in Wardour Street – a location that somehow manages to feel both expensive and slightly down at heel, the buildings just a little too tall for the width of the roadway. The street was still in shadow, though the morning was well advanced.

The building itself was thirties art deco, recalling a time when this had been a rather glamorous part of town and the hub of a British film industry that thought it had a real chance of rivalling Hollywood. The decor of Dennis's office made no concessions at all however to the elegant and now fashionable chrome-work and graceful curves. He clearly had his own idea of faded grandeur based on a house that he had possibly visited or (for all I know) burgled many years before.

From the moment we entered the room, I could see that Elsie was determined to be impressed by nothing that Dennis had to show her – not the large mahogany-and-leather partner's desk, not the massive leather sofas, not the shapeless pieces of modern statuary, not even the richness of the carpet (the impossibly deep pile of which made the long walk from the door to Dennis's desk an entirely silent one). Elsie had elected to wear on this occasion a very tight short skirt and matching jacket, which might have looked good on a number of people. There was undoubtedly, somewhere inside Elsie, a thin fashionable woman trying to get out, and you could only admire her tenacity.

Dennis extended his hand to me. 'Sorry to hear about Geraldine, old man. Very tough on you.'

I shrugged. 'There's a lot to sort out,' I said.

'Of course. And I'll be delighted to help in any way that I can. But first, would you both like coffee or something stronger?'

It was ten o'clock in the morning, so it must have been a safe bet that neither of us would opt for a whisky. But perhaps other morning visitors to this office did.

'Coffee, please,' I said.

'Me too,' said Elsie. She had not taken her eyes off Dennis since entering the room and was now fixing him with a stare. If it was intended to intimidate him, however, it was not working.

Dennis spoke into an old-fashioned microphone beside his desk, and coffee and biscuits appeared almost immediately.

'So tell me,' he said, 'what exactly is it that I can do for you both?' He smiled an expensive gold smile.

'There are one or two things that it would help me to know,' I said.

'Fire away. Anything at all.'

'Very well. You had some contact with Geraldine before she disappeared?'

'A bit.' The smile remained but his manner became guarded. 'I didn't know exactly who she was when she first contacted me. She was just somebody who had a proposition for me – I get lots of those in my line of business.'

'Which is . . . ?' said Elsie.

'This and that,' he replied blandly. 'As I say, I get a lot of propositions, but this one seemed sound enough and to involve no risks – for me at least. Geraldine wanted to invest in some property in the East End, do it up, sell it on to the gentry – such as our good selves.' He smiled again. 'She wanted me on the board as an adviser. I was most happy to help her. She didn't ask me to put money into the scheme – not that I would have, of course. I expect my capital to earn twenty-five, thirty per cent a year. At the best she was going to make fifteen with the market as it was. Maybe twenty with my advice and a following wind. Of course, she found a way to make a hundred per cent, but I didn't know then that she was going to split with the whole bundle.' Dennis chuckled approvingly and took a sip of his coffee. 'Good coffee this. I have a little man who imports it directly from Costa Rica for me. None of your Fair Trade nonsense – he rips the Costa Rican peasants off a treat. I'll get you some if you like. At cost, obviously.'

'When did you find out who Geraldine was?' I asked.

'When she chose to tell me, I would imagine.'

'The name meant nothing to you before that? Elizabeth hadn't mentioned it?'

'Possibly – I really don't remember. Look . . . the fact that Geraldine had run off with Elizabeth's ex might have been significant to the memsahib, but for me this was strictly business, old man. Strictly business.'

It occurred to me then that the only two people who called me 'old man' were Dennis and Rupert. There were patterns everywhere. Rupert dropping one blonde to go for another. Elizabeth moving effortlessly from one poseur to another (admittedly very different). You could not avoid the conclusion that Dennis had at some stage in his life invented himself from scratch every bit as much as Rupert had. What were the patterns in my own life? Whom did I resemble? I preferred not to think about it.

'There must have been a risk that Elizabeth would find out,' observed Elsie. Her need to make herself heard had finally overcome her desire to put Dennis in his place.

Dennis gave a half-grin. I guessed that, like Geraldine, he thrived on risk. As such, it would have been a mutual bond and attraction. But Dennis, unlike Geraldine, would have wanted the risk to be defined and controlled.

'Does Elizabeth know?' I asked. 'What would she do if she found out, I wonder? What if somebody who knew were to tell her?'

'Who's going to do that?' he smiled.

'I might.'

'Now hang on, old man . . .' Dennis started to say. This was clearly one direction that he had not expected the conversation to take. He was becoming irritated, but he was becoming worried too. I didn't look like a blackmailer, but then he didn't look like a crook (or so he imagined anyway).

'Yes,' I went on. 'I *could* tell Elizabeth. Why not? She's a good friend of mine. You've already said that you knew she wouldn't have approved. You could say that it would be my duty to tell her.'

'But you wouldn't?'

'Maybe,' I said, aware that Elsie had switched her gaze to me, and was now staring at me as though I had started to do a strip-tease while humming 'The Teddy Bears' Picnic'. But I pressed on. I knew what I was doing. (At least I hoped that I did.) 'The police haven't included you in their investigations, either. After all, nobody has told them about your connection with Geraldine. You never can tell.'

'Don't try to blackmail me, Ethelred. Others have tried before. I'd get you to have a word with them so they could give you a bit of advice, but you might have some difficulty tracking them down.'

'This isn't blackmail.'

'Well, what do you want then?'

'All I want is for you to answer three questions for me. If you answer them truthfully then neither Elizabeth nor the police will hear a word from my lips. But if I ever find out that you have lied – ever – I will make two short phone calls. Do you understand me?'

'Sure.' Dennis was less certain than ever what to make of me, but had decided that, for the moment at least, the best policy was to play along. Unlike Elsie he was not looking at me as though I was crazy.

'First question. Do you know what happened to Geraldine the day she disappeared?'

'No, of course not. I was in . . .' Dennis consulted a diary (leather-bound, obviously). 'Strasbourg. Yes, I had a whole series of meetings there. Elizabeth came too. But she told you, surely? I know that I hadn't seen Geraldine for weeks before that. She was losing interest in actually buying property. Well, we all know why now, don't we? But even at the time it didn't strike me as odd that she hadn't phoned or anything. The project was making no progress. Mentally, I'd already written it off.'

'Thank you.'

'Well, if that was your first question, it was hardly worth blackmailing me for. You could have had that for nothing.'

'I wanted the answer to come with a cast-iron guarantee. Second question. Did you ever sleep with Geraldine?'

'What?'

'Did you ever sleep with her?'

'No.'

'Did you want to?'

'Is that the third question?'

'No, still the second.'

'The answer is still no. Oh, she was attractive. Of course she was. And I don't doubt . . . well, you of all people would know what she was like. But that would have been one risk too many. I suppose that Elizabeth has already told you about

Cathy – our last nanny? I thought so. Well, I've no intention of putting myself in that position again. Elizabeth would take the kids and take me for every penny I've got. I'm getting too old to throw everything away for a quick leg-over. Satisfied?'

'Yes.'

'Third question?'

'I don't need to ask the third question,' I said. 'I already know that you don't have the answer.'

'Can I ask what the third question was?'

'No,' I said.

'Then can I ask you one?'

'Certainly.'

'Who do you think killed Geraldine?'

I paused for thought. 'I think the police have got it right – they are looking at a serial killing.'

'So, she was about to do a runner and ended up in the wrong place at the wrong time?'

'I don't know anything about the details,' I said.

'So, who took the money out of the account, then?' interjected Elsie.

'What account?' asked Dennis, suddenly interested.

I silently cursed Elsie's scatter-gun approach to questioning, but this was an aspect of the case that we were going to have to explore with him. I therefore explained about the Swiss account, the whole time carefully watching Dennis's face to try to tell whether he possibly knew even more.

Dennis nodded approvingly at the efficiency of the operation and then leaned back in his chair and took out a cigar. He cut the end carefully. 'I don't see any problem there. From what I've heard, no papers were found with the body – no passport, no driving licence, no cheque-book, no credit cards?'

'That's right,' I said.

'There you are then. She must have had details of the Swiss account on her too. If there were passwords, she probably had them written down somewhere – most of you mugs do. The chappie who does her in goes through her papers and realizes that he has all he needs to collect the cash, if he moves quickly. He hides the body well enough, and removes anything that might help identify it, to slow things down if it is discovered. He heads off for Switzerland, passport and bank details in hand. Bingo!'

'He,' said Elsie. '*He*. There's going to be a problem when he presents the passport at the bank and claims to be Geraldine.'

'How much was in the account?' asked Dennis.

'Six hundred thousand,' I said.

'Francs?'

'Pounds.'

'No problem,' said Dennis. 'That would split very nicely two ways. Plenty of blonde girls in Switzerland to choose from.'

'Geraldine had an accomplice in England,' said Elsie. 'I'm sure of it.'

'Who is doubtless keeping very quiet at the moment,' said Dennis. He lit the cigar and blew out several large puffs of smoke. 'Case solved.'

'Could be,' I said. That at least was something that Dennis and I could agree on. Dennis had his reasons for wanting the world to lose interest in the murder of Geraldine Tressider, just as I had mine.

'Funny blokes, serial killers. I knew one in Chelmsford,' said Dennis, watching his cigar smoke curl up into the air and slowly drift away.

'Chelmsford?' asked Elsie.

'He was in Chelmsford nick,' said Dennis thoughtfully. Both his accent and vocabulary had relaxed a little during his discussion of the murder. Now, just for a moment, a heavy curtain blanketing the past seemed to have been twitched aside. But just as quickly its folds swung back again. The light that had gleamed briefly was extinguished. The old manner and accent reasserted themselves. 'You meet some odd coves in my line of work, of course.'

'Which is?' asked Elsie.

'A bit of this. A bit of that,' he replied. 'More coffee, dear lady?'

Twenty

It was shortly after that meeting that Elsie made a strange remark to me, though perhaps with hindsight it did make some sense.

· 'Elizabeth never did have an eye for the genuine article, did she?'

'Dennis, you mean? No, he clearly isn't what you might call out of the top drawer.'

'Dennis and Rupert.'

'Rupert?'

'My old man knew Rupert's old man quite well.'

'In Southend?'

'They were both in the same business – fruit and veg.'

'What, you mean that Rupert's father ran a fruit-and-vegetable stall?'

'Maybe not that. He was apparently quite well off as these things go. But he used to do business with my old man, so he wasn't exactly the Duke of Westminster. He used to give my old man credit, so he wasn't exactly Albert Einstein either.'

I did not try to argue with her, though I later wondered

how Elsie's father, who had probably never met Rupert, could be so certain that it was Rupert's father that he had met and done business with. That his father might have made his money from fruit and vegetables added yet another side to Rupert's character, but it did nothing to solve the more immediate problems that confronted me.

But the meeting with Dennis had cleared up one doubt in my mind. It had, if you like, closed one of the many doors that had been annoyingly open when the policeman first brought me the news of Geraldine's disappearance. My problem now was that I had been too successful in ruling out lines of inquiry and had left myself nowhere to go. There was one vital piece of information I still required, but it seemed that I would have to wait for that to come to me – if it ever chose to do so.

The police investigation too seemed to be losing the brisk momentum with which it had began. Nobody now searched Cissbury Ring for clues, and the remnants of blue-striped tape had vanished from the gorse bushes. Contact with the police became, for me, a rarer event. My brief notoriety in the village too had come and gone. The few people who knew I had any connection with the case (and nobody in Findon had ever met Geraldine in real life) had ceased even to comment on the bizarre coincidence of her death. I had been told that I would need to attend a coroner's court, then that I would not be needed after all. I was told that the police would soon have further information, then heard nothing from them for weeks. I was still a step or two ahead of the police, but it was doing me no good.

I did not expect the case's appearance on television to take things forward, nor do I think it eventually did. But that evening I naturally felt obliged to be in front of my television set in Findon, as I knew Elsie would be in Hampstead. Geraldine's last known movements and the finding of the body were reported in detail, with just a few significant facts withheld, as I believe is customary in these cases. (Fairfax would have no truck with the media, so appeals to the public via the television are an aspect of police work that I have never researched.) The presenter made it clear that the police saw this as just one of a series of murders committed in West Sussex, and ended by appealing for information concerning the whereabouts of Mr George Peters, who the police thought might be able to help them with their inquiries. Mr Peters was urged to contact them if only to rule himself out of the investigation. ('Oh, right,' I thought. 'I'm sure he'll be only too happy.')

Of course, it was not the only case featured that evening and again I was struck by the patterns, the coincidences. There were strange parallels, for example, in another case – one Mary Jones of Margate, whose face now appeared on the screen, smiling shyly. Miss Jones too had had a failing business, though in her case it had been a design consultancy. On the day of her disappearance, she had visited Bournemouth to make a presentation to a company that she hoped would offer her some work. She was deeply in debt and this was, acquaintances had darkly told the police, a meeting that she saw as her last chance to save her business from failure. She had arrived in Bournemouth by train and allowed ample time for a meeting that she expected might take two hours; it had in fact been curtailed after fifteen minutes. She was informed that her approach was not one that would suit the client concerned: they had no wish to waste any more of her (or their) time. She thanked them politely and left, saying that she would perhaps visit a local art gallery before catching the return train. She was never seen again, other than the obligatory blurred image on a security camera in a department store. A little later £400 was withdrawn from her bank account in two separate transactions using her cash card.

She had no close family and, it seemed, few friends. It had been over two weeks before anyone even thought to report her missing. We had been treated to a few charming shots of Bournemouth, but now Mary's picture was flashed up on the screen again. Had anyone seen her on the day of her disappearance in September or in the weeks that followed? She smiled at us out of the television, in a picture taken at a party perhaps or on a rare day out. 'I'm probably dead, but please don't trouble yourself on my account,' it seemed to say. You felt that this lightly freckled face could have been quite pretty, given even minimal effort, but the long mousy hair did not flatter her, nor did her lack of make-up. Her dress, as far as one could tell, looked drab and old-fashioned. You could almost see her at the presentation: shy, diffident, lacking in confidence, bound not to succeed. In one small vignette you saw an entire life of humiliating failure. 'Where did she go after the meeting?' asked the presenter. Had we seen her? Could we help? But you could have passed her a dozen times in the street without noticing her. So, no, probably not.

There were three others who had also vanished without trace. Wayne, a wannabe actor, had left home for London and never reported in. Single mother Paula was believed to be sleeping rough in the Manchester area without single baby

Tiffany, who awaited her return. Ada, nice old dear and sufferer from Alzheimer's, had not been seen by neighbours for two weeks and was believed to have wandered off to her ultimate doom and destruction. Had we seen them? Could we help?

All four pictures appeared again, each occupying one-quarter of the screen – four total strangers juxtaposed for an instant in time. A number to ring was flashed up, partly obscuring Wayne and Ada, who had drawn the short straw and chanced to comprise the bottom half of the picture.

Then it was on to a shocking case of the impersonation of a gas-meter reader in Sevenoaks; and Wayne, Ada, Paula and Mary were returned to the back burner.

The phone rang and I knew that it would be Elsie.

'Well?' she said, getting, as ever, straight to the point.

'It won't help,' I said.

'She wasn't murdered by a serial killer,' she said. 'I'm certain of that. You know it, too. Remind me again why you told Dennis the Menace that you believed the police version?'

'Because it really doesn't matter who it was,' I said.

'How can you say that?'

'It's true. It doesn't affect anything.'

'I've been thinking, Ethelred, shouldn't we tell the police about the Swiss bank account at least? I know that it would be embarrassing for Smith – but that can scarcely worry you. I suppose that it might also mean the creditors get their hands on the money and Rupert will lose out too. But neither of them are exactly deserving cases. Quite the reverse – next to Geraldine, the two of them must have done you more harm than anybody. Surely you can't feel any need to protect them?'

'The harm that has been done cannot be undone,' I said. 'None of it.'

'You're in a cheerful mood tonight.'

'Programmes about crime do that to me.'

'Don't have nightmares,' said Elsie.

'I won't.'

But all that night, whenever I closed my eyes I saw the sad, haunting face of Mary Jones – the long mousy hair, the freckles, the apologetic smile. What had been in her mind the day she disappeared? Was she, like Geraldine, planning to vanish quietly and start afresh elsewhere?

In the grey half-light of a winter dawn I went to the cramped little room that serves as the kitchen to my flat and made myself a cup of coffee. Then I sat there alone, sipping it very slowly.

Twenty-one

Feuillet sans date

Something has happened to me; I can no longer doubt it.

The change has not come suddenly. Indeed it has come so slowly that even now I am unsure when the process began, if indeed it can be called a process. But I am aware that things which were once familiar to me now look strange and unnatural.

Take my police notebook for example. To all appearances it is much as before – a simple spiral-backed A6 block with a stiff blue cover. It sits in front of me on my desk as it has, and many others have, before. It is a notebook with sixty or seventy pages of ruled paper. That is all. It is the most ordinary thing imaginable, an object that is so insignificant as to be almost unnoticeable. Yet I am afraid of it.

No, not afraid. How can one be afraid of a notebook? But simply to view it fills me with loathing. If I touch it, I know that I shall feel warm bile rising in my throat; the room will begin to dissolve. The cover of the notebook will be rough and dry as old parchment. It will crumble in my hand. It is a thing utterly alien, subtle, menacing in its impermanence.

So, is it that this notebook has changed subtly over the past weeks and months? Have my desk, my chair, my carpet assumed new characteristics without my being aware of what was happening? This is improbable. But, if that is so, then I must accept that I myself have changed, that I am less myself than I was before. In which case, who am I now?

Outside the sun is shining on the green fields. I can see trees, a river, some cattle. Yet, even as the ideas form in my mind, I realize the words themselves have lost their meaning. Very well, then. I need to try to analyse what I see, what I feel. If I had to define what is in front of me, I would say that it is a fine day in July and that the scene is a typical English country landscape. Nothing wrong with that. Why then does this too make me feel nothing but nausea?

It is true that I am subject to sudden change. There was a time when I drank heavily, even at the office. Then one day I simply stopped – for a while at least. My interests have changed too. At about the same time that I stopped drinking I developed an interest in Norman architecture that absorbed me totally. Why?

Perhaps if I record day-by-day what my feelings are I can record the nuances, classify them, make comparisons. And yet at the end, I know what lies at the bottom of it all is [word left blank in the manuscript].

3 heures et demie

Three thirty. Too early to do anything, too late to do anything. I shall have to wait until evening comes. Then we shall see. But in the meantime I remain slumped in my chair, too enervated even to turn away from the objects on my desk which so disgust me.

I can only just see from my window the awning of the Cathedral Tea Rooms, yet I can hear, from behind their lace curtains, the unmistakable sound of ragtime music building slowly to a crescendo. I know this record well. In another few seconds the negress will start to sing. It is inevitable, unavoidable, and absolutely necessary that this should happen. For an instant the music ceases, then her voice cuts through the hot afternoon air:

> *Some of these days*
> *You'll miss me honey!*

This is true, I think. Some of these days you'll miss me. That at least is a certainty.

Edit.
Select All.
Delete.

Twenty-two

I can no longer remember precisely why I chose the latter part of the fourteenth century for my historical novels. It was as good a time as any, and nobody had done it recently – not as detective fiction, anyway. Today of course a new writer of historical whodunits would find that there were few empty slots in the calendar, but I was in there early enough to stake my claim to Richard II and to mine that slender seam of gold for what it was worth. It has been worth four books so far. Like so many other things in my life, it could have been worse.

All ages, if you examine them closely enough, prove to be periods of transition. Nothing stands still and each century is (depending on your viewpoint) a dusty trackway from the last or the green lane leading to the next. Or whatever. But the late fourteenth century . . .

Though few at the time had yet noticed, large cracks were starting to appear all over the proud but grubby facade of feudalism. Soon the tidal wave of the Peasants' Revolt would surge up from the coasts of Essex and Kent, until it spilled over the walls of London and gurgled into the stinking River

Fleet. And though it would all trickle away again with the ebb tide, it would leave a strange and unfamiliar landscape in its wake, smelling of fresh salt air and dead fish: a rich soil in which all manner of unexpected things might grow, given time.

Of greater interest to me as a writer was that, in that same fertile landscape, French was giving way to English as the language of literature. A certain Geoffrey Chaucer was busy at his day job in the king's service, while turning out the occasional poem.

I originally had the idea of making Chaucer the central character in the novels – the first was to be called *Inspector Chaucer Investigates* – but, once the novelty of Chaucer as a policeman had worn off, there seemed little more to the joke than that. I eventually came up with a minor official in Chaucer's office: Master Thomas, a failed physician employed as a clerk, who was able to use both his position at court and his medical knowledge to solve the crimes that occurred with surprising regularity (two and a half per book on average) in and about an otherwise dull customs office. I came to the books with no preconceptions about Chaucer's character, other than to be vaguely well disposed towards a fellow writer. Viewed from Master Thomas's eyes he rapidly became a loathsome windbag, driving his staff to exhaustion, belittling all literary efforts except his own and flaunting his tenuous links with the aristocracy. He was also a plagiarist. Many of his finest lines proved to have been stolen from Master Thomas, who was also unwise enough to share with Chaucer his plans to write a book about some pilgrims going to the shrine of Our Lady at Walsingham. ('Canterbury,' said

Chaucer with a condescending smile. 'In spite of some passing resemblance to the modest little manuscript that you showed me, my own work concerns *Canterbury*. Another place entirely, my dear Master Thomas. Now, what were you saying a moment ago about April showers?') One feature that Thomas shared with Fairfax was that he received almost no credit for his efforts, literary or detective, and looked fated to remain for ever a clerk in the Customs House. For a while I feared that Master Thomas would merely become a fourteenth-century Fairfax, but he remained obstinately chirpy and shared none of Fairfax's introspectiveness. Nor, surprisingly, did he share Fairfax's interest in church architecture. In the fourteenth century Perpendicular was replacing Decorated as the dominant style, but Thomas declined to make any observations on the subject other than to note, on a visit to Canterbury Cathedral, that the remodelling of the nave was producing an unreasonable amount of dust.

I think that I was attracted to the period above all, however, by the character of Richard II, who also made several appearances in my books. Richard was a man born out of his time. He would have made an excellent Tudor. He would have passed unnoticed in a whole crowd of Stuarts. But he simply could not hack it as a Plantagenet. A later age would have understood why he wished to appoint ministers who were loyal to him personally rather than merely loyal to their class. A later age would have agreed that it was not an important role of a king, still less an essential one, to lead troops into battle. A later age would have understood a king's wish to be a man of learning and a patron of the arts rather than a soldier. A later age might even have understood his ideas on the nature of kingship. The fourteenth century just looked at him as if he had farted and offered the throne to Henry IV, a man who knew how to wield a sword and who said 'lavatory' rather than 'toilet'. Richard II had all the right ideas at the wrong time. Did he interest me in spite of his evident failure or because of it? Again, I would not care to say. The investigation of his lonely death (from starvation in all likelihood) was to be the next of the Master Thomas stories. Of course, I knew that I would never write it now. Just as I would never write another Fairfax novel, however hard I might try.

Twenty-three

Fairfax stood by the side of his desk and surveyed his office.

'Pathetic,' he said. 'That's what it is. Pathetic.'

He walked round to the other side of his desk and again surveyed the room.

'As I thought,' he said. 'No better from this side. But do they care? Oh no, that wouldn't be politically correct, would it? Pathetic, that's what it is.'

There was the sound of the door opening behind him.

'Good morning, Sergeant Fairfax,' said Constable Pooh.

'Good morning Sergeant Fairfax,' said Constable Piglet.

'Good?' said Fairfax. 'Yes, I suppose that it is good for some people, Constable Piglet. Good for muggers, I would imagine. Not bad for drug dealers, paedophiles and teenage delinquents. I expect that they are all having a lovely time, and (don't get me wrong) I'm very happy for them and for all their social workers. But there are *some for whom it is not as good as others. I'm not com-plaining. But that is how it is.'*

'Is something the matter?' asked Constable Pooh.

'Matter? With me, Constable Pooh? Why should you think that?'

Constable Pooh considered this for a moment. He put his head on one side and then, since that did not seem to work, he put it on the other. Then he looked up at the ceiling.

'Precisely,' said Sergeant Fairfax. 'All around me you can see the many things that I have to be happy about.'

Constable Pooh looked round the office again and then under the desk. 'Where?' he asked.

'Can't you see them? Promotion? The esteem of my colleagues? The support and respect of a grateful public? A top-of-the-range sports car? Heaps of banknotes? Joie de vivre? (That's French for sex, by the way.)'

'No,' said Constable Pooh. 'No, I can't.'

'Neither can I,' said Fairfax. 'Odd that. You'd have thought after a lifetime with the police force, a lifetime of selflessly fighting crime, I might have had just one of those. Two would have been nice, but I would settle for just one.'

'I think that I had the respect of the public once,' said Constable Pooh, 'but I must have mislaid it somewhere. I will ask Christopher Robin.'

'You are a policeman of very little brain,' said Fairfax. 'That is why they all run rings round you: the villains, the leftie politicians, the interfering do-gooders who wish to defend the civil rights of a criminal to commit crimes

unharassed by the likes of you and me. You go out on the beat with both arms tied behind your back and then they criticize you because old ladies are getting mugged on their way to church by youths who have bought their knives with social security money. Crime doesn't pay? Don't make me laugh. We're just on the wrong side.'

'I thought that criminals were on the wrong side of the law,' said Constable Pooh.

'Not any more. We're the ones to be watched now. We're the ones to be monitored. Forget catching villains, Constable Pooh. If you want promotion, just meet your equal opportunities targets.'

Pooh was not sure what to reply to this and so just hummed to himself for a while.

Buckfordshire, Buckfordshire, Buckfordshire pie
A lie can't kill, but a killer can lie
Ask him who done it and he'll reply:
Buckfordshire, Buckfordshire, Buckfordshire pie

At the end of the first verse, Sergeant Fairfax had not actually flung him out of the office, so Constable Pooh sang the second verse, but very quietly and just to himself:

Buckfordshire, Buckfordshire, Buckfordshire pie
She's def'nitely dead, but we don't know why
So go and ask Tressider and he'll just reply:
Buckfordshire, Buckfordshire, Buckfordshire pie.

'Tressider!' muttered Fairfax. 'I shan't be working with him again.'

'Why not?' asked Constable Piglet.

'Why not? How should you know a thing like that, good trusting little Piglet? You do not yet understand the evil of this world or the duplicity of writers. But he knows why not. He knows what he's done. Oh yes, he knows what he's done, all right. Don't you, Tressider? Don't you, Tressider, you criminal?'

Edit.

Select All.

Delete.

'I had no choice,' I said to the blank screen. 'I couldn't have done anything else. And I was in *France*, dammit.'

Still, it would not be long now. There was that consolation. It would not be long now.

Twenty-four

They buried her in December. For a long time they would not release the body, but then, just before Christmas, we were finally allowed to lay Geraldine to rest.

I had assumed that she would be buried in the churchyard at Feldingham, possibly alongside my old buddy and college friend, Pamela Hamilton-Boswell. Ethelred announced however that Geraldine had always expressed a firm desire to be cremated. This surprised me in that A) Geraldine never planned anything that far ahead and B) even if she had, she was not one to contemplate her own death for long enough to express any wishes at all. Still, Ethelred had undeniably been married to her and it was not impossible that they had amused themselves on rainy afternoons by discussing each other's funerals. And who was I anyway to express an opinion as to whether the Bitch should burn or rot? Both were fine with me.

So, on one of the rare bright sunny days that winter I found myself driving rapidly (I was late, naturally) back into the wilds of the Essex marshlands. My new black skirt was slightly too tight for effective gear changes, but the roads were empty and wound undemandingly through the flat countryside and towards the sea. The midday sun remained obstinately low in the sky and cast long shadows over the ploughed fields. But it was a cheerful scene, with light strangely reminiscent of a summer morning.

The crematorium was in one of those pretty but over-formal parks that fool nobody into thinking they are anything other than what they are. The big chimney belching black smoke is always a dead giveaway, in my opinion. The good old funeral conveyor belt was operating nicely, with one jolly little party emerging from the back door as ours was entering at the front. I parked my VW next to a large new BMW with immaculate black paintwork and tan hide seats (Dennis had made it to his former business partner's send-off, clearly) and set off at a brisk but ladylike pace so that I'd make it before the coffin did.

My father was the youngest of a large family, so I've been to the funerals of assorted relatives over the years and am used to the routine. A bloke with his collar on back to front goes, 'I am the resurrection and the life, saith the Lord,' and a few old dears snivel. You kneel down, stand up, sing, wonder whether you remembered to lock the car, sit down, pick your nose, think, 'It's a sodding crematorium – nobody's going to nick a car from *here*,' stand up, sing again, and that's about it, really. Piece of piss. Unless you're the corpse.

Since I was at the back of the chapel I could amuse myself by counting the mourners (twenty-two actually) and trying to identify their backs. The camel overcoat (a bit too pale, a bit too flash for a funeral) was Dennis. The shabby black duffel coat was Rupert. Ethelred was in the front pew with Charlotte, both in newish black suits. The two old biddies in Gawd-help-me hats next to them would be aunts or something. I couldn't place the worried-looking slap-head just in front of me, except that his pinstripes marked him out as being not from these parts. Darren Oxtoby was over to the right and I managed to catch his eye and give him a smile and a nod. Oh yes – didn't I say? – he was one of my authors by that time. Of course, he sent in the complete manuscript rather than the first chapters and summary that I had so clearly requested. (Writers? Can't fart without an agent to remind them where their arses are.) But hey! – the manuscript was good. No, really, really good. From the very first page, I knew that I could sell it. It was a Gothic fantasy, but told with such humour and such a lightness of touch that it was like nothing I had read before.

After the service was over we all trooped out of the side door so that the next lot could come in the front ('I am the resurrection and the life, saith the Lord,' stand up, sit down, etc.). We all shuffled past the vicar and muttered, 'Lovely service, Vicar, deeply moving.' We gave our condolences to Ethelred and Charlotte, on the grounds that there was nobody else to give them to and we didn't want to take them home with us. Then we were out in the fresh air and the bright sunshine. Nothing like a funeral for making you feel really alive. We all milled around for a bit, admired flowers and told each other that it was brass monkeys right enough.

One of the main problems with a cremation is that there is no grave to dance on afterwards. Still, I had a spring in my step as I headed back to the car park. We'd cremated her. It would be interesting to see how the Bitch wriggled out of that one.

Everyone was invited back to Feldingham – a good fifteen-minute drive along narrow roads. As we passed the little parish church, the perversity of travelling miles to an anonymous crematorium struck me again. Somewhere in that decision there was a clue to how

Ethelred felt about Geraldine, but whether it was a final act of love or a final act of revenge beat me.

Not, as I may have observed before, that I know a great deal about love. My old man once said to me, thus combining sex education and his philosophy of life into one short lecture, 'Elsie, just you remember this. Love is sad; sex is funny. If you find you're crying, then either you've just caught your finger in the mangle or you're in love. If you find you're laughing, then check your knickers out, because you could be having sex.' He was as pissed as a newt when he said it, but it stuck in my mind.

I suppose that that's one thing Ethelred and I have in common – fathers who were total prats. It's a bond of sorts. It's one of the reasons why I like him. He's OK – I mean OK for an author, obviously. There's also something about the way he stands there all hunched up like a droopy penguin. Well, they're an endangered species or something, aren't they? You can't help feeling a bit protective.

Most of those who attended the funeral showed up at Charlotte's for salmon-and-cucumber sandwiches and mince pies (it being almost Christmas). The slaphead took the first opportunity to go off with Ethelred for a private chat. He returned looking grey and corpse-like himself.

'Well, thanks for *trying*,' I heard him say, and recognized the flat, tired voice as that belonging to Smith-the-Bank. He looked in my direction. Of course he had no idea who I was or that he'd ever spoken to me. I smiled at him, thinking how, with that oily skin and those thick, blubbery lips, he was even more unattractive in the flesh than he had been on the phone. I got no response to my smile, however. His face was blank and if it conveyed anything it conveyed utter despair. Had I been a painter it might have appealed to me as an allegory of greed and lust getting its just deserts, but I'm not a painter, so it didn't appeal at all.

I caught Ethelred's eye and he winked back at me, then went off to talk to Charlotte. Suddenly I felt snubbed – almost jealous, though there was clearly no reason to be anything of the sort. If Ethelred and Charlotte wanted to do the host and hostess bit, like an old married couple, it was no skin off my nose. One of Ethelred's problems is the way he just lets women push him about. I wouldn't stand for it if I was him. I really wouldn't.

I grabbed Darren by the arm and took him out into the garden for a largely unnecessary chat about royalties. I came back to find Ethelred talking to the two aunts, which was all right if that was what he wanted to do.

'Greetings, dear lady,' said a voice behind me.

'Good to see you, Dennis.'

'Not a bad joint for a modern box,' he said, looking around, 'but I prefer something a bit older and more upmarket. Take my place for example – Grade Two Star . . .'

'I've seen it,' I said.

'You'll know what I mean, then,' he observed with a passing sneer at the light fittings.

'Yes,' I said. 'I do know what you mean. Can I ask you a question?'

'Of course. Can't guarantee I'll answer it, though. Ha ha.'

'How easy is it to get somebody bumped off?'

Dennis considered this without any sign of surprise. 'May I ask who you are planning to have killed?'

'I'm asking on behalf of a friend.'

'Yes, people always do. Obviously it can be done if you have the contacts. How much do you want to pay?'

'I like to get value for money. So does my friend. Who's doing special offers on bumping off your nearest and dearest?'

'You're after the cheapest? The price of some junkie's next fix, dear lady. But don't expect that one to remain your little secret for very long. When you pay a real professional, what you're buying is a discreet personal service with no comeback. And that's not cheap.'

Even at the time, I suspected that Dennis was bullshitting and knew no more about it than I did, but it sounded convincing. The fact that he was a shady geezer in a flash overcoat gave him a certain amount of credibility in this respect.

'Tens of thousands of pounds?'

'Ten thousand, say. But he didn't do it.'

'What do you mean?'

'What you really want to know is: Did Ethelred hire a contract killer? Right?'

So, actually, Dennis wasn't so stupid, really.

'And?' I said.

'Most contract killers would use a gun. Some might use a knife. I've never heard of one strangling somebody with their bare hands. Why bother? Too slow. Too crude. Too uncertain. To strangle somebody like that would just show a lack of planning. It wasn't a contract killing.'

'Well done, Dennis. That's a weight off my mind, I don't mind telling you.'

'Unless they wanted to make it look like a serial killing, of course.'

'Oh, right. So, I'm back to square one. Thanks a bunch, Den.'

'Ethelred's not a killer – either in person or by proxy. I know that and you know it too. Anyway, what's it to you?'

'I don't like losing one of my authors. I'd rather they stayed out of jail.'

'That's all there is to it?'

'Yes, Dennis. That's all there is to it.'

'If you say so. He's a good man.'

'I know. He always said that he never knew what Geraldine saw in him, but I do. He is a good man. He's dependable and kind and trustworthy. Of course that sort of thing can get right up your nose. Dependability is something that you only appreciate as you grow older. So I can see why Geraldine might have wanted a break from it but I can equally see why, after a few years of Rupert, she might have wanted him back. He'd have gone back to her too, the silly bugger. Geraldine's death was one of the best breaks Ethelred had.'

'Just another of your authors then?' He raised an eyebrow.

'Thank you for the advice, Dennis,' I said.

'Don't mention it, dear lady.'

I went in search of more tea. As I passed the two aunts, I heard one say to the other, 'But *murdered*, my dear. Surely nobody else in the family has been murdered?'

'Ivy,' said the other.

'Oh, but that was by her husband – quite a different matter.'

'I suppose so,' said the second aunt. 'I didn't see him at the crematorium, did you?'

'No, he doesn't get about much now, poor man.'

I passed on, still tea-less.

Rupert was talking to the vicar. He is the sort of person who knows how to talk to vicars. It's a gift; either you have it or you don't. He saw me, disengaged himself from the clergy (an even greater gift in my view) and came across the room.

'Hello, Elsie.'

'Hello, Rupert. How are things?'

'Well, frankly, not too good. There doesn't seem to be a lot of work around for fund-raising consultants at the moment. Geraldine clearing off with the cash has really finished me off. The landlord's not too happy at not having his rent paid on the nail. I asked Ethelred if it wasn't time to go to the police – they might just be able to trace whoever withdrew the money from the bank in Switzerland. He reckons that the other creditors will just swipe it if we do – you know, the banks and people. He says it's better to track down the cash ourselves. But what if he can't? I mean . . . I might have to get a real job.' He laughed, which under the circumstances could not have been an easy thing to do. 'Ethelred will get the money, though, won't he?'

Well, I'd seen desperate people before, but nobody so desperate as to pin their last hopes on Ethelred Tressider.

'Yeah, sure,' I said, sounding more like the kind, reassuring Ethelred Tressider every minute. 'Of course he will.'

I finally caught up with Ethelred as most of the other guests were leaving.

'Nice skirt,' he said. 'New?'

'A bit tight,' I said, giving it a tug. 'They tried to sell me a size sixteen, but I wasn't having any of that.'

He nodded sympathetically, but what would he know about how we women are made to suffer?

'How are things?' I enquired, the way you do.

'Geraldine's estate is almost wrapped up,' he said. 'I've sold the flat. Completion's not until the New Year, but everything's sorted out. Nothing left for me to do – the lawyers will sort out the last bit.'

This struck me as odd, in the sense that up until then he'd

insisted on handling everything himself. But if he wanted to take a break and let some solicitor do it, fair enough.

'Fair enough,' I said.

There was one of those pregnant pauses, then he suddenly blurted out, 'Elsie, can you do me a favour?'

'Maybe,' I said – though obviously I was going to do it, whatever it was.

'I've got some stuff I want you to look after. It's in the car.'

The 'stuff' proved to be two large boxes.

'What's in them?'

He pulled one open. It was full of manuscripts, packed tightly in two piles. On top were the typescript of *All on a Summer's Day* and a few pages of messy, childish handwriting.

'All the early ones are there on paper,' he said. 'The later ones are on disk.'

I reached into the box and took out the slim handwritten effort.

'"The Penkwen and the Hedhog?"' I said.

'That's "The Penguin and the Hedgehog",' he said, hunching his shoulders and shuffling his flippers a bit. 'It was my first novel. I was six when I wrote it.'

'I should hope so. Penkwen? I have to point out that there is usually no W in "Once upon a time" either. Who was your editor in those days? OK, I'll take care of the manuscripts. What's in the other box?'

'This and that. I'm trusting you not to peek. I can tell you, however, that at the very top is a letter to be opened in the event of my disappearing and not coming back.'

I felt a cold shiver. What the hell was he on about?

'Where are you planning to disappear to?' I demanded.

'I don't know yet.'

'So why might you not come back?'

'I don't know that either.'

'Ethelred, is somebody threatening you? Is somebody blackmailing you? Look, if they are, Dennis may know what to do. I'll speak to him if you don't want to.'

'Oh, there's no danger at all,' he said. 'Not for me, anyway.'

He smiled confidently, the way he had in the car on the way back down to Sussex, just before the police arrested him.

'Right,' I said. 'Whatever you say. And in the meantime, you want me to look after this stuff?'

'Yes. Until I am able to send you other instructions. Keep it safe and don't even open the second box unless you need to. Can I trust you?'

'Ethelred, I don't understand this and I don't like it.'

'Can I trust you?'

'What do you think?'

'Thanks, you're a star, Elsie.'

'I know,' I said.

At the first layby outside Feldingham I stopped and opened the second box. Well, come on, what would you have done? It contained mainly photograph albums with, tucked away down one side, some pieces of jewellery. I flicked through a couple of the albums. There were old pictures of Ethelred, pictures of Geraldine, one or two of a much younger Rupert and lots of a whole load of people I didn't know from shit. One album was devoted just to Ethelred and Geraldine's wedding. I was in one or two myself. Jesus, what did I look like in that lemon frock with half of Kew Gardens attached to my shoulder? (You might not think it now, but I used to have this really crap taste in clothes.) And there was Ethelred, grey morning suit, top hat and a bitch on his left arm, smiling sweetly. Round her neck was a gold chain that was, incidentally, one of the pieces of jewellery tucked away in the box.

On top of all of this was a sealed letter. I looked at it and ran my finger along the top. It would be the work of a moment to tear it open. But then I thought, No, he trusts me not to. How can I yield to temptation within minutes of leaving him? I'll wait until tomorrow for the letter.

So what was I to make of it all? The pieces of jewellery might technically form part of the estate, but he had probably bought them for her and, in his shoes, I would have tried to claw back some of the cash that she'd walked off with. But the photo albums? Of course, I could understand why he might have seen them as something that was irreplaceable and why he might have wanted them, along with the manuscripts, to be in safekeeping. But why shouldn't I see them? They were only photos, after all. Or was it a double bluff? He obviously knew that I would open the box and *wanted* me to see the albums. I couldn't help feeling that I was being presented with clue after clue, but was failing to fit them together. In Rubik's cube terms, I was back to six sides all looking like rainbows.

I shut the boxes and drove west, back to civilization. The knowledge that the letter lay, still unopened, in the second box gave me a feeling of virtue all the way home.

Twenty-five

The public soon lost whatever interest it had had in the murder of Geraldine Tressider. The killing of a little Nigerian boy in south London hit the headlines soon after and stayed there most of that winter. Mary Jones, the sad management consultant, had her brief moment of fame when the police announced that, in the absence of any sighting since her disappearance, they were now treating the case as a murder inquiry. But in view of the absence of a body or anything else, her case too faded from sight as a wet November turned into a wet December and our minds turned to serious problems, like how to keep the diet going over Christmas. I never did find out whether Wayne, Ada or Paula were heard from again. Not everyone who goes missing wants to be found. Geraldine, of course, had not wanted to be found either – only the silly cow overdid it as usual.

For a week or two after the funeral, I saw little of Ethelred. He was busy with various things and I suddenly had my hands full with an auction for Darren's novel, which resulted in an advance large enough to make the inside pages of the major dailies. Then Ethelred vanished to spend Christmas with some distant relative in Dorset.

It was funny the way that I missed him now when he wasn't around, but I reckoned I'd see plenty of him in the New Year.

As for me, I spent the festive season alone in Hampstead – not as bad as you might think in that nobody gets drunk and storms out of the house, and you get to watch whatever rubbish on TV takes your fancy. Well, I'd opened my present to myself (chocolate), one from Ethelred (chocolate, bless him) and one from Darren (chocolate), eaten Christmas lunch (microwaved turkey, chocolate, plus half a grapefruit to show the diet I hadn't forgotten it) and settled back for a mindless six hours of prole-feed on the box, when it occurred to me that there was one little treat that I'd been saving up, to wit, Ethelred's farewell letter. It was the work of a moment to retrieve it from the box and there it was in my hands, quite unaccountably open.

Dear Elsie [it read], I assume that you will read this in the first layby you reach on the way home. [That's all you know, I thought.] Well, that's fine by me. I can't yet tell you where I am going, because I don't know and so you're none the wiser. What I do know is that, one way or another, I will be off on a long trip sometime next year – call it research for my next book if you wish. Before I get down to detail, I want to thank you for all the help you have given to me over the years and for the help that I know you are going to give me.

Oh right. I am, am I?

There then followed detailed instructions for the payment of royalties into his bank account, a list of standing orders that had been set up, what to tell the neighbours, what to do with his car and so on. Three pages in all, and each as dull as the one before it. He'd thought it through like the tax inspector he still was, at heart. Bless.

But no instruction to go to the police and tell them the Mob was after him. No instruction even to go to the police and tell them that Geraldine had been ripping off all and sundry. No confession of anything at all.

I suppose my feelings on getting to the end were, as I have so often felt at Christmas, that it had all been something of a let-down. I knew very little now that I didn't know before, except that Ethelred's heating system had a seven-day timer and that his car insurance was with the Civil Service Motoring Association, neither of which facts was exactly riveting. But it served to remind me that the core to the mystery – the nature of Ethelred's Quest – was still unsolved. From the moment he returned from France, nothing he did had really made sense and in spite of my best efforts as a herring seller's apprentice I really had no better idea now of who had killed Geraldine or what Ethelred had had to do with the business than I had at the start.

Then, in that terrifying, yawning gulf between the Queen's speech and the earliest you can decently go to bed, I had one of those ideas that I just knew I would end up regretting. France! Yes, of course, that was the line of inquiry that I had overlooked. If I was to understand Ethelred's actions all that autumn, surely the key to it lay in his trip to France? Was it a coincidence that he was away when Geraldine disappeared, or had it all been planned? Wasn't the logical conclusion that I should get on over to Châteauneuf-sur-Whatever and *check it out*? Well, I should think so. I looked at the map. There was the choice between an orange *autoroute* heading unerringly south via Paris or an elegant arc along various red *routes nationales* down through the Pas de Calais and Normandy. I instinctively went for the scenic route. It's amazing how many crap decisions you can make in a single evening if you put your mind to it.

I suppose that I started to have real reservations as I manoeuvred the car off the Shuttle at Calais and noticed that people seemed, for some reason, to be driving on the wrong side of the road. This clearly was not going to be a trip on which I could allow my attention to wander.

I'd timed it all so that I would do most of the drive overnight and have the roads to myself – another of those things that seemed a good idea when I thought of it, but less good now I looked through bleary eyes at the traffic streaming south into the darkness.

It was somewhere around Abbeville that it occurred to me that my motor insurance probably didn't cover me for this trip, and just outside Rouen that it struck me that it might have been advisable, in the holiday season, to pack some French money with me in case the banks were closed. I stopped at a place advertising itself as Louviers and tried my bank card in a hole-in-the-wall machine, fully expecting it to vanish without trace, but the machine delivered a hundred euros. Feeling that I was on a winning streak, I stopped again at Evreux and, in a brightly lit but deserted square, drew out two hundred. I wasn't sure exactly how this trip was going to turn out, but I reckoned that I would need all this cash and more before it was over.

After Evreux the roads became eerily empty for a bit and I developed a tendency towards what I can only describe as sleep-driving. I flashed through shuttered villages where every living thing seemed to have vanished behind the stone and half-timbered walls. With me on the road this was a wise move. From time to time a massive lorry travelling in the other direction would dazzle me with its headlights, then I would be left alone to drive on the right or left as I thought best.

At Verneuil (scene of an English victory in 1424, as I am sure you will know) I realized that at the last junction I had completely lost the concept of a left turn and that, if I was to finish the trip alive, I needed rest. So I parked at the first layby, locked the doors and crashed out for a few hours. I awoke to grey skies, a gentle French drizzle and the knowledge that I still had some way to go.

Six chocolate croissants and a cup of coffee at Châteauneuf-en-Thimerais restored my belief that life was worth living and I pressed on southwards towards Orléans. I reached Châteauneuf-sur-Loire in the late morning, and quickly identified the hotel at which Ethelred had stayed.

It was on the river but in all other respects it was a right dump. Old chintzy wallpaper, sun-bleached mahogany, heavy velvet curtains and a funny smell dating back to the fifties. Under the circumstances there was nothing for it but to hold my breath, check in and then proceed with my investigations as best I could. I spent most of a leisurely lunch thinking through possible strategies, but without coming to any definite conclusions other than that I was obviously a total dickhead to come here at all. Still, nothing ventured and all that.

I waited until after dinner that evening, when the reception desk was quiet and nobody much was around, to engage the receptionist in conversation.

I asked him for a stamp as a plausible pretext for approaching him. He obliged, letting me offer in return the comment that it was very pleasant here in Châteauneuf-sur-Loire, to which he was pleased to shrug in a Gallic manner, intimating that he did not give a shit what I thought about anything. I smiled my best and sexiest smile. My friend Monsieur Ethelred Tressider had recommended the hotel, I said. Perhaps he (the receptionist) recalled Monsieur Tressider? He said, '*Paf*,' or something of the sort, adding that the Old Bill had been round asking questions. He seemed particularly proud of knowing that *les flics* were called the Old Bill in English. A graduate of the Dennis Rainbird School of Languages, no doubt. And what, I wondered, had the Old Bill asked him? Not much, just to confirm the dates of Monsieur Tressider's stay, which he was content to do. That was all. '*Paf*,' he observed again to nobody in particular.

Well, we were getting on like a house on fire and no mistake, so I asked him to suggest a few things I might do in Châteauneuf and its environs. What, for example, had Monsieur Tressider done? He had, it seemed, spent a great deal of time out on the terrace with his portable computer. He had been very content to sit and write. He had been working on a new *roman* with which he had been very pleased. It was crap, I said. Dog crap. '*Merde du chien*?' he repeated slowly, clearly a little puzzled, in spite of my uncanny grasp of French idiom.

'Forget it. What else did he do?' I asked.

Monsieur Tressider had apparently also visited a number of châteaux. *Hélas*, they would be closed at this time of year but the art gallery would be open at Orléans and possibly the local museum of cheese and viticulture. He had details somewhere. He would let me have them tomorrow morning.

He seemed ready to finish the conversation at that point and turn his attention back to his magazine, so I tried another line of questioning: Had Monsieur Tressider received any visitors while he was at the hotel? A lady perhaps? The concierge stiffened considerably. Certainly not, he said. At the Hôtel Printania down the road such things might be arranged, but his was a respectable family hotel. No, I said, nothing dodgy – just a friend from England passing through, perhaps? A blonde bitch with freckles? Nobody, he said. He was alone all the time. Did anyone phone him? I enquired.

Now he did more than just stiffen. He carefully folded his magazine and looked me straight in the eye. Why did I want to know? The implication was that, whatever my reason, he wasn't planning to tell me until I told him what I was up to.

A range of possible lies occurred to me, some more implausible than the others. I selected one at random. I was, I said, a private detective employed by Monsieur Tressider's wife. Monsieur Tressider was suspected of infidelity and I was here to gather what evidence I could. If there was some small charge for supplying the information, I would be happy to pay. Quite why I decided to say this was not entirely clear to me, except that it was much more straightforward than the truth and I had most of the necessary French vocab for it.

At first I thought I had made a major error because, when I spoke of marital infidelity, he seemed inclined to side as a matter of principle with the unjustly accused husband. But fortunately the word 'pay' immediately appealed to his finer and nobler instincts. He scratched his nose and looked me up and down, as if assessing what he could sting me for. So, what did I need to know?

Did anyone phone Monsieur Tressider? Did he phone anyone? Well, said the concierge, it would be difficult, against hotel regulations and contrary in all likelihood to the Code Napoléon, but it might be possible to check outgoing calls. How much dosh did I have in mind? I suggested one hundred euros. He said, '*Paf.*' I said one-fifty and he said that he would, in return for the money in advance, let me see all of the records of Monsieur Tressider's stay. If I went to my room he would bring them up to me when the coast was clear.

He arrived twenty minutes later with a ledger and a beer, the delivery of which was to be his pretext for coming to the room if anyone asked. I said that I did not like beer. He shrugged and sat there drinking it himself, the froth decorating his moustache, while I read what papers there were.

The bill detailed the usual extras and impositions of hotel life – newspapers, bar bills, dinners most evenings, and just two tele- phone calls, apparently charged at the usual hotel rate of about a zillion euros a minute. Both calls were to the same number in the UK – a fifteen-minute call and a much shorter call almost immedi- ately afterwards. And the date was the evening before Geraldine's murder. Even as I looked at the paper, I felt that here was a genuine clue staring me straight in the face. I went through the bar bills and so on once again, not because I expected to find anything, but because I'd paid almost a hundred pounds for this and wanted to get my money's worth. Then I scribbled down the number – the only bit of evidence I'd gained – signed a chit for the beer I hadn't ordered and told the receptionist that he might now piss off and spend his ill-gotten gains.

After he had gone, I sat looking at the number. There was the UK code, then there was 20, so this was a London number. The next bit, 7607, was, as far as I remembered, an Islington prefix. Of course, if I really wanted to know whose number it was, there was one way to find out without further delay.

Unlike Ethelred, I did have a mobile that worked outside Sussex, though doubtless I would be charged large numbers of euros for daring to use it on the wrong side of Calais. Still (as I may have observed in the past) nothing ventured and all that. At the far end the phone rang six times.

Then there was a click and then a dead person spoke to me.

'You have reached Geraldine Tressider. I am afraid that I can't come to the phone right now, but if you would like to leave a message I will get back to you as soon as I can.'

Well, that's a trick I'd like to see, I thought.

There was a beep at the far end and I left a recorded message of ten seconds of heavy breathing before I realized that I was still pressing the phone hard against my right ear.

There were clues here staring me in the face. I knew Ethelred had only just sold the flat, and that it was still empty, but why had he not cancelled the phone ages ago? Why could I still get Geraldine's answerphone? What exactly was the advantage of keeping that going?

It was an interesting question, but it didn't really lead anywhere, so I took my emergency chocolate from my bag and flopped down onto the hard hotel bed. I unwrapped the bar and, though this was usually a sacred moment for me, took the first bite almost without noticing what I was doing. So, what did I now know that I had not known before? Ethelred had phoned Geraldine the evening before she was killed. Twice. One short call, one long one. What did that mean? It meant if nothing else he could have known her plans – precisely where she would be the next day at what time. But what had he done next? There was no subsequent call to the hit man in London, which was good news. On the other hand he could have gone out to a phone box or sent an email from an Internet cafe, so that really proved very little.

One short, one long. It was like Morse code. One short, one long. I stared at the ceiling repeating the words to myself until I drifted off to sleep, but awoke the following morning eight hours older and no wiser. I pulled back the curtains. The dawn was grey and rain was falling softly on the Loire Valley.

Twenty-six

The journey back along the orange *autoroute* was a piece of piss, though the traffic around Paris was interesting. All the way, the rain lashed down and the windscreen wipers swished and I thought of those two phone calls. I stopped only for lunch in an anonymous service station, where I had *moules frites*, and was back on the proper side of the Channel by late afternoon. Just over two hours later I was in Findon, ringing Ethelred's doorbell and getting no reply. Then, and only then, did I remember that he was supposed to be up in Scotland, teaching on some jolly New Year writers' course. The fee on offer had been good and Ethelred had, unusually, been keen on the cash. It looked like being a wet and dreary trek back to town.

But first, yes, obviously, chocolate.

The lights were still on in the post office, which seemed a good place to re-stock before starting home. I had become quite a regular customer there and could have located what I needed blindfolded if necessary. Karen, the owner, had been about to close up, but she kindly waited while I chose the largest bar I could find and paid for it.

'You'll have heard the news, then?' she asked as I handed over the coins.

'News?'

'They caught the man who murdered Mrs Tressider,' she said. 'Sort of.'

So, I thought, I've driven over a thousand kilometres to the Loire and back, only to find that all of the action has been going on in Findon. Brilliant.

'What do you mean – sort of?' I asked.

Karen showed me a copy of the *West Sussex Gazette*. 'Murder Suspect Killed in Car Chase,' said the headline.

'The police spotted his car in Findon Valley,' said Karen. 'He made a run for it. You know that sharp bend by Windlesham House School? Apparently he tried to take it at a hundred and twenty miles an hour, and that was that. In the end they had to identify him by his dental records.'

'And ...?'

'It was that Peters fellow that they'd been looking for.'

I bought the *Gazette* as well as the chocolate – not that it would tell me much more than I already knew, but I felt that at this moment I needed hard facts to keep me going. Had I only known, I had a whole mass of facts hurtling in my direction. So, under the circumstances, I could have saved myself 37p, but nobody ever tells you these things until too late, do they?

The following day I went for an early-morning walk on the Heath, something I almost never do on the grounds that just looking at the joggers makes me feel shagged out. They were there in force that morning, splashing along the paths in their Day-Glo winter Lycra and Nike gloves. (You wouldn't credit what some people wear.) The dog people were there too, walking their Labradors and poodles and terriers, clutching their green bags of poop – like badges of good citizenship. What with the joggers and the dog-walkers there was hardly any space left for normal people to walk and think.

Back at my flat I went through Ethelred's boxes again. There were the manuscripts. I laid them out on the floor, but they were just as he had said – paper versions for the early novels, disks for the later ones. Also the one about the penkwen. No extra clues there. Then I looked at the jewellery. One or two nice pieces, that gold chain for example, but for the most part nothing of any great value. Geraldine had presumably taken the better stuff with her, and it had vanished with everything else. What was left was the sort of thing that you hang onto for sentimental reasons, but most of which should have now found its way into some charity shop rather than Sotheby's. Geraldine might have wanted them during her lifetime, but why was Ethelred hanging onto them?

Finally, I went through the photograph albums one by one. There were the early ones, with a youthful-looking Ethelred and a smiling Geraldine by his side. Then some that were clearly later. Snaps of an older Geraldine. Geraldine with Rupert. Rupert with somebody else. Rupert and Geraldine at somebody's wedding. Rupert on his own.

But of course. These were not Ethelred's photograph albums at all. They were *Geraldine's*. So why would Ethelred give me these rather than his own for safekeeping? I could see their value to Geraldine while she was alive, of course, but they would mean nothing to Ethelred. Why would he want them now that Geraldine was dead?

I don't know if you do jigsaws, but there is always a stage where you would swear that the morons have left a piece out yet again. You search through the box, but nothing looks even vaguely like the bit you need. Then you pick up a bit you knew you had all the time, turn it round, and suddenly Bob's your uncle. It was just like that now. The piece I had needed was sitting there all the time, just waiting to be seen the right way up.

Yes, why should anyone want them *now that she was dead*? A cold chill ran down my spine. And at that moment, for the very first time, I knew exactly what Ethelred had been playing at.

The silly tosser.

Twenty-seven

All that afternoon and most of that evening I tried phoning Ethelred's number over and over again. Somewhere in Sussex a phone rang in an empty room and stopped. Then it rang again and stopped again. Then it rang. I am sure the neighbours loved it, but into the life of every Sussex village a little rain must fall.

It was almost one o'clock in the morning when the phone was finally picked up and somebody said, 'Hello?'

'Ethelred, you tart, I've been trying to phone you all day.'

'I've only just got back from Scotland.'

'Well, you took your sodding time.'

'Possibly. Look, is this urgent?'

'No, I always phone people in the small hours for a casual chat, dickhead.' It's not only Swiss banks that can do irony. Bearing in mind that I should have been asleep just then, I was not doing it too badly, either.

'Well, what is it then?'

'We need to talk.'

'Generally or specifically?'

'I need to stop you making the biggest mistake of your life.'

There was a pause and then Ethelred said, 'I've got a plane to catch.'

'In that case I'm coming right over.'

'Now?'

'When else? Now. Listen, Ethelred, I know everything. You've finally slipped up. I know exactly what your game is, you pillock.'

There was another pause. 'I doubt that,' he said.

'I know who you're off to meet.'

'Do you? I bet you don't.'

'You bet I do,' I said. 'The only thing I don't quite understand is how you've got away with as much as you have.'

'Unmerited good fortune,' he replied. 'And the fact that I'm a writer of detective stories. That I suspect played a large part in It.'

I may have given a snort of derision at this point.

'You're right,' he continued, 'perhaps that was not significant. But it has gone much better than I could have possibly hoped. I've had two massive strokes of good fortune – Peters's death was the second, of course.'

'Of course,' I said.

'After all, it would have been most inconvenient if he had been able to deny that he had ever met Geraldine.'

'Very. But why did you do it?'

'I suppose that I never stopped loving her.'

'A tosser to the end,' I said. 'What time does your plane leave?'

'I have to check in around five o'clock.'

'In the afternoon?' I asked hopefully.

'In the morning. The taxi's booked for four.'

'Cancel it. She's just using you, Ethelred.'

Another silence, then: 'All right. I'll tell you what. Perhaps you do deserve an explanation, at least. We'll talk about it all on the way to the airport. I'll tell you what happened and if you can make me change my mind, I won't get the plane.'

'Don't leave until I get there.'

'I promise.'

'Good. But honestly, I despair of you. Ethelred Tressider, what are you like? Eh?'

'I'm like my father,' he sighed. 'I'm exactly like my father.'

Another bizarre night drive, but this time primarily on the left-hand side of the road. I passed through the weird, empty, ochre, neon-lit City, over Blackfriars Bridge and along the South Bank. The Houses of Parliament appeared briefly across the dark water on my right, the long blank wall of Lambeth Palace on my left, and then I was off into the unending grot of south London. Somewhere around Chessington I hit open country again, and it was foot down on the accelerator, slamming on the brakes only momentarily for known speed cameras. Michael Schumacher would have been proud of me. Him and David Attenborough. This was, after all, a mission to Save the Penguin.

There was a note on the front door of Greypoint House that read, 'Don't ring – door unlocked – come straight up.' Kind of him to think of not disturbing the neighbours, I reckoned. Well, some prat had apparently kept them awake until one o'clock in the morning ringing the phone.

When I entered the sitting room, three cases were standing neatly packed in the middle of the floor. Ethelred was tidying some papers away.

'At least you're still here, you pillock,' I said.

'I am a pillock of my word. I never tell a lie.'

'But you tell the truth pretty selectively.'

'That's what writers do. As you will recall, I am a writer. To be exact, I am three writers,' said Ethelred.

'Then you'd think that one of you at least would have some sense.'

'What are you saying? I'll never get away with it? That was one cliché I did manage to avoid putting into the mouths of any of my characters.'

'No, I'm saying you are a complete dickhead.'

'All right. So tell me what you think you know.' He gave me a funny look. If it had been anyone except Ethelred, it might have frightened me. But it was Ethelred. Just dear old Ethelred the Penguin.

So, I gave him the lot, finishing with the telephone call from France, the yellow dots, the photograph albums and the jigsaw analogy. Though I say it myself, I was shit-hot stuff.

'Not bad,' he said when I had finished. 'There is some detail that you have missed – but then I don't know the whole story myself, of course. I promised to tell you on the way to the airport, and so I will tell you everything I know. The taxi is cancelled, by the way. We'll take my car. If you don't make me change my mind, you can drive it back from Gatwick for me, OK?'

'OK,' I said.

Ethelred smiled. 'Good. That's settled then. Now, we've got a few minutes to spare. Would you like some coffee?'

I shook my head.

He looked a little disappointed. 'What about some hot chocolate then? I've got some Charbonnel and Walker's.'

He knew that there are certain things that I cannot resist. 'Just a big one then,' I said.

I drank it while he got together the last few things he wanted to pack. The hot chocolate was really very good. Once or twice I thought that it had a slightly bitter aftertaste, but I drank it all. Obviously.

Twenty-eight

Are you sitting comfortably?

Another journey in the rain, I'm afraid, Elsie. It's enough to make you want to leave the country, eh? The trip should take no more than forty minutes – but that should be enough time, I think, to give you the full story. The corner we're coming up to now, by the way, is the one where Peters crashed. They've removed the wreckage, of course, but you can see the spot in our headlights now – look, just there where the earth's ploughed up and the grass is scorched. A hundred and twenty miles an hour? Not even his Porsche could manage that. We'll take it at a slightly more sedate fifty, I think. We've plenty of time. All the time in the world, really. Well, you have anyway. Just settle back and listen for a bit. Heating too warm? No? Good.

   If there's one thing I tried to avoid in any of my books it's long concluding chapters in which everything is explained. But you deserve the complete version, so forgive me just this once.

You are right in thinking that you have worked out some key elements in the plot, but that of course was your difficulty all the way through – you thought that it was just *one* story, whereas in fact it was three, linked only in the most tenuous way. To use your analogy, you had the pieces of three different jigsaws in your box, and that's why you've been struggling to make sense of them.

So which story shall I begin with? How about Mary Jones's story? It's a rather sad little tale, but perhaps the most straightforward of the three. So, yes, let's begin with that one.

You will remember Mary Jones from *Crimewatch*: the rather plain lady consultant who vanished in Bournemouth. Of course, I don't know all of her story and the only people who can fill in the missing details are dead, I'm afraid. But we do know that she was a rather unhappy and lonely person, with few friends, a failing consultancy business and a large overdraft. She arrived in Bournemouth one day towards the end of September to pitch for some work with a company there. She had, you will recall, allowed a couple of hours for the meeting, which in fact ended after fifteen minutes. Poor Mary. She must have realized that she was on the road to bankruptcy. So what did she do? Oddly enough, I can tell you almost exactly. She did not visit any of the local galleries. She did what any self-respecting woman facing bankruptcy would do – she went shopping. First she went to one of the department stores – she was caught on camera there. (Fame at last, eh?) She bought a bright red Italian suit. Then, at the same shop or elsewhere, she bought some expensive Italian shoes. She paid cash, withdrawn from a cash machine that day. I suspect that she had no choice but to pay cash, because her Access card had already been taken away from her, but that's just speculation on my part. She probably also bought some new lipstick and eye shadow; I don't think that she had owned either of these things before and she would certainly use both before the end of the day. Finally, she went off to a hairdresser's and had her long mousy hair cropped short and dyed blonde. The makeover was complete. Did she feel better for it? Did she have a new confidence that everything was going to be OK? I hope so. I do hope so.

Then what? I have to start guessing at this point, but it goes something like this. She finds a cafe somewhere near the railway station to wait for her train. She orders a cappuccino and pays with her last remaining banknote. She pockets the change and sits, aware that a man at the next table is eyeing her appreciatively. This never happened before the makeover. She glances briefly in his direction: he's rather good-looking. Dark wavy hair and a gap between his front teeth. He smiles at her. She looks straight ahead of her again, not in fact totally displeased, and takes a sip of her coffee. She takes out the novel that she has brought with her – *Professional Misconduct* by Amanda Collins – and pretends to read about the exploits of the dashing Mr Colin Cream MBBS FRCS FDSRCS (Eng).

Then suddenly there he is, standing at her table – not Colin Cream, but somebody almost as good.

'Don't I know you from somewhere?' asks the man. (Let's call him George Peters, because that was his name.)

'I don't think so,' says Mary. It's an obvious chat-up line, but Mary doesn't get chatted up too often.

'Your face is very familiar. Do you work for the BBC?'

'Me? No! Do you?'

'Oh yes. I'm a producer,' he says.

Yes, OK, I really am making the dialogue up now, but something of the sort *did* take place somewhere in Bournemouth that afternoon. Maybe he didn't then offer to buy her another coffee – perhaps it was a glass of Chardonnay or a half of lager. Maybe he told her he was a professional footballer or that he was in advertising. But let's stick with coffee and the BBC for the moment.

So, Mary drinks her second coffee and they chat for a while.

'Do you live in Bournemouth?' asks Peters.

'No, I'm just here on business. I'm getting the next train back to Margate.'

'Really? What a coincidence. I'm going that way myself this afternoon,' says Peters, his eyes opening just slightly too wide in surprise. 'We're filming near there tomorrow. I could give you a lift. Forget the train. You can travel by Porsche door to door.'

'Don't be silly – I've got a return ticket.'

'Throw it away.'

'What a waste! I couldn't!'

'You could. Honestly, it's going to be faster than having to change trains in Portsmouth and Brighton, or wherever it is. And anyway, I'd really enjoy your company.' He smiles. There's that gap between the teeth again (just like Colin Cream). He looks nice.

Funny, with hindsight, to think that with her long mousy hair and no make-up he would have ignored her completely, and she would now be alive and bankrupt and asleep in a single bed in Margate. But Peters likes blondes. I mean, *really* likes blondes. So what happens is this.

'If you're sure . . .' she says.

'Oh, yes, I'm sure.'

She smiles too. She in her turn rather likes this dark-haired man – so different from the librarians and accountants that she has (only very occasionally) been out with before. There is just a hint of danger about it all – a hint of danger that the new Mary in a bright red suit feels is rather fun. 'So this is what blondes get up to,' she thinks.

Then off they go, along the south coast on a sunny September day. Does she enjoy speeding along in a sports car? Does the wind blow through her new blonde hair? Do they stop somewhere later for a drink or a candle-lit supper? Again, I really hope so. It would be nice to think that she was happy on her last evening.

Somewhere near Worthing they turn off the main road.

'Where are we going?' she asks.

'Have you ever seen the moonlight on Cissbury Ring?'

'No.'

'It's magic. Really romantic. I'll show you. It won't take long.'

Romantic? Yes, please, she thinks. I like romantic.

The moon is bright. The car speeds along the Sussex lanes. This, thinks Mary, makes up for everything else. This, in my new Italian red suit and my new red Italian shoes, is the beginning of a new life. The life I was always meant to have.

At what point, I wonder, did she realize that it was all going horribly wrong? On the muddy climb in those new red shoes up to the top of the hill? Or not until his hands closed round her throat? Poor Mary.

Now, unlike Mary, I am back on firm ground again. The following day a man walking his dog finds the body in a depression that was once an old flint mine. Nearby is a damp copy of a cheap romantic novel.

A little while afterwards Mary is lying on a table in a brightly lit room that is all white and chrome, not that she is in a position to notice her surroundings. A middle-aged gentleman, who would have been a total stranger to her in life, comes in. He is accompanied by a young policeman. They are in their different ways apprehensive about what they have come to do. The young policeman is not used to this type of work. He is uncomfortable with the dead and even more so with the bereaved, and he just wants it to be over as quickly as possible. The middle-aged gentleman's worries are less easy to pin down. When he sees the body a look of shock momentarily passes across his face, then he smiles.

The policeman notices neither reaction. He wishes to catch nobody's eye for the moment. 'We immediately assumed that it was your wife,' he says. 'But we do need you to confirm the identification.'

'I see,' said the gentleman.

'So, you are able to identify the body, sir? I understand that it's been some time . . .'

'I would know my wife anywhere, officer,' says the gentleman quickly and firmly. (It is true, he would – though, as it happens, this is not she.)

'You've no doubt about that?'

'None at all.' (This too is true – he is certain that, if he ever saw his wife, he would know her. Anywhere.)

The young constable breathes a sigh of relief. 'We are very grateful to you for identifying the body, sir. I realize that you and she have been divorced for some time. We might have asked her sister, but she does live some way away and it would have been . . .'

'Very distressing for her?'

'Exactly, sir. Very distressing.'

The conversation continues for a short time, then, at the young constable's suggestion, they leave, and the sound of their voices fades away down the long corridor. The lights in the room are switched off and Mary is left alone again, as she was for so much of her life. Some time later she is cremated under the name of Geraldine Tressider, but that is to jump ahead in our tale.

OK so far, Elsie? Are you beginning to feel sleepy? I'm not surprised with all the driving you've done over the past few days. Tip back the seat if you like, you'll be more comfortable. Just listen to me droning on and to the hypnotic swish of the windscreen wipers. That's right. Close your eyes if you like.

So, who next? I think it must be time for Ethelred Tressider. You may remember him too? A hack writer of no importance. Three hack writers, to be precise. Let's tell his story.

At what point did I realize that I was turning into my father, I wonder? There was no sudden revelation on the road to

Damascus. For a long time, in fact, I truly believed that I was doing what I had always wished to do and had the respect and, up to a point, admiration of my peers. I wanted to be a writer and that was what I was. It was only over the years, as the prizes failed to come in, as the reviews (good or bad) became shorter and less frequent, as even the local bookshops stopped inviting me to sign books, that I gradually became aware of ambitions that would never be fulfilled: aware that there are . . . well . . . writers and writers. On a good day, Elsie, I obviously blamed you for luring me from the straight-and-narrow path of true literature in pursuit of a modest but comfortable income. But on a bad day, I knew that I had nobody to blame but myself. Like my father I was living a mere caricature of the career that I had intended, becoming more and more ridiculous as the years went by: a strange stooped figure, whom the village children would advise to get a life, since it was so obvious that I did not have one. It is said, Elsie, that Cardinal Newman, having left the Church of England and met with nothing but reverses in the Church of Rome, was one day found silently weeping outside the church at Littlemore, where he had in happier times been the incumbent. I never returned to bestow my tears on the railings of the tax office, but I would sometimes wonder whether I might by now have been a senior inspector of taxes and I would note, with a strange fascination, each civil service pay increase.

I suppose that I might have continued, almost indefinitely, prodding an increasingly reluctant Fairfax into action once a year, alternating this with a tale from the ever-fascinating world of oral and maxillofacial surgery. Master Thomas would have investigated the strange death of Richard II, and perhaps entered the service of the House of Lancaster. The wily and untrustworthy Henry IV would have had a use for him. He might not have been too old perhaps to accompany Henry V to Agincourt in some capacity. For him, unlike Fairfax and me, all sorts of opportunities beckoned.

Slowly, I began to form a plan. I would *break free*. One day I would simply vanish, taking with me nothing but my laptop computer and a change of clothes. I would starve in a garret and write a masterpiece. So what stopped me, Elsie? The practicalities of it all, I suppose. Of course, it was an attractive idea: walking out one early summer morning, the misty sun just a finger's breadth above the horizon, with nothing but a knapsack and the dusty open road ahead. But I would leave behind a tangle of unpaid bills, mortgages and standing orders. There would be books that I would miss, pictures, photographs – all becoming damp and mildewed in an empty flat. I wanted to flee and become a different person, but the person that I was said I couldn't go.

Then Geraldine came back. She arrived on my doorstep quite suddenly one morning and announced that we were going to have lunch together. That I might have anything better to do would not have occurred to her. She knew that there was nothing better to do than have lunch with her on a fine spring morning.

And suddenly I was eighteen again.

She never explained why she had come back, she never apologized for any minor inconvenience she might have caused me in the past – that would have been totally unlike her. In fact she began, over that first lunch, to describe her latest project, suggesting casually that I might like to invest several hundred thousand in it. When I said that I did not have hundreds, let alone hundreds of thousands, to spare, she burst out laughing and said that that was as well, because I would never have seen the money again. She then described how she planned to milk a number of mugs of whatever she could get, before fleeing the country and her accumulated debts. It was an amazing act of trust, under the circumstances. It was one of her random moves, and she sat back to see whether I would take her queen or resign the game. But, of course, she knew which I would do.

I told her that I had also thought of vanishing without trace, and ran through the photograph-album aspects of it. I had expected her to mock me, but she became serious and agreed that this would be difficult. Unless one had an accomplice to sort out that sort of thing, I said. We both looked at each other and I knew that I had just been recruited as an accomplice. And I didn't mind. It was like being back at school, and finding that you had just been picked for the first eleven. It was like your publisher phoning you up and telling you that you had been shortlisted for the Booker Prize. It was better than both: I had been picked as Geraldine's friend.

We didn't sleep together – not that time anyway. But halfway through lunch she suddenly asked me, 'Are you wondering whether I still wear black underwear?' I denied it, and may have even blushed. She laughed and said, 'Well, you'll have to use your own initiative to find out the answer to that one, won't you?'

When she left for London she kissed me on the cheek – a simple act but one that seemed to promise an infinite range of future favours. The last trace of her perfume seemed to linger about me for the rest of the day. Any reservations that I might have retained vanished. I was seduced.

And on later visits . . . well, like Amanda Collins, I'll just have to leave you to fill in the details for yourself. She does still favour black underwear, by the way.

Most of that spring and summer we worked on the plan, adding elements here, refining details there. A great deal of time was spent on agreeing where Geraldine would flee to. I concurred that Brazil might be suitable. I raised only minor doubts over Bolivia. It was only when we started discussing Belgium, Botswana, Burma and Bhutan, that I realized that Geraldine's approach remained alarmingly random. At a very early stage it was agreed that, having covered up her disappearance, I would come out and join her and we would sit admiring the Andes (or Himalayas or Ardennes) and I would write my masterpiece. We debated for some time whether she should slip away quietly and unobtrusively (my plan) or whether there should be a more dramatic display with suicide notes and piles of clothes left discarded on a remote beach (Geraldine's plan). This small detail was unfortunately never entirely resolved – to my satisfaction anyway.

But in the meantime, we set about constructing a new identity for Geraldine. Obtaining a passport in the name of somebody who died as a baby – a real person with a real identity but no further use for a passport themselves – was my little contribution as a novelist. It is a well-known device from detective fiction. Indeed, so well known is it that checks are now carried out by the Passport Office using parish records. As a result a cottage industry has grown up, stealing parish records to prevent such investigations. And of course, as Charlotte told you, the parish records had, quite coincidentally, been stolen from the church in which Pamela Hamilton-Boswell is buried. Pamela's history was well known to Geraldine. As long as nobody had already used her, we were safe. They hadn't. The passport came through and 'Pamela' vanished off to Switzerland for a couple of days to open a bank account.

Geraldine refused to let me have anything at all to do with the matter of raising capital, other than to promise that she would steal only from people who she was sure could afford it and that I would not like. That she chose Rupert, Smith and her sister Charlotte was, in a funny sort of way, her apology for walking out on me. She was offering me a chance of revenge on those who had mocked, reviled or otherwise incommoded me all those years ago. All very *Count of Monte Cristo*, eh, Elsie? What she overlooked of course was the fact that, whenever I read that book, I always feel sorry for Baron Danglars and the others long before the Count has completed their ruin. I did try, but I have to admit that I took relatively little pleasure from the discomfort of my erstwhile enemies – except Smith, perhaps, once or twice. But Geraldine did it for me, and I appreciated the kind thought.

We agreed that it was essential that as little suspicion should fall on me as possible, and I therefore arranged to be out of the country on the day she was to vanish. The night before her departure, even though I had agreed not to contact her at all, I phoned her from my hotel. I just needed to hear her voice. It was a mistake. Inevitably we argued. She had decided to go for the dramatic gesture: a suicide to be faked in much enjoyable detail, including a car abandoned on a remote beach. I pointed out the inadvisability of drawing the attention of the police to her disappearance before she had had a chance to ensure that she and the money were completely untraceable. She said that I always spoilt people's fun, and we inevitably began to rake up much past history, in the way people do when they have a lot of past history to rake up. She hung up on me. I phoned her back. The answering machine had been switched on. She was uncontactable.

I reassured myself that this was only a temporary tiff. She would phone me in England, from Bolivia or Bhutan or Belgium. But no call came, only a policeman to announce her disappearance.

You were right about my reactions. Of course, I showed no surprise at all when he announced that her car had been found abandoned: I never doubted that she would press ahead with some idiotic scheme. But I had assumed that the plan had been to leave behind her own car, not a hire car . . . and above all it would be left well away from Sussex to avoid any hint of involvement on my part. Clearly she had made an extra few thousand on the sale of the Saab, but at what risk to the credibility of her disappearance? Then there was the ridiculous 'suicide' note. Of course I saw, even from the photocopy, that she had used a sheet of my writing paper, and I wondered what on earth she was playing at. Was she getting back at me for the phone call? Was it some sort of joke? Or were these more of her random moves, just to see what might happen? Or was it a straight double-cross?

The more I thought about it, the more likely the double-cross looked. After all, she was prepared to deceive Rupert,

Smith the bank manager, Charlotte and goodness knows who else. Why not me too? Her claim to be exacting some sort of revenge on my behalf looked with hindsight more like a way of salving her own conscience as she defrauded people of their cash. Yet even in my darkest moments, I never quite lost faith in her – soon she would phone me and all would be well.

Then came the news that a body had been found. As I drove to the police station I was quite confident that the police had made a mistake but then, just for a moment, in that white room I really did think that it was her. The short fair hair and the freckled face gave much more than just a superficial resemblance. Had I not seen her for ten years, I might have actually believed that it was Geraldine lying there. So certain were the police that they had found her that I was already relishing the prospect of telling them how wrong they were. But another thought entirely occurred to me. If they wanted to believe that this was Geraldine, why not let them, at least for a while? After all, I could always claim later to have been quite reasonably mistaken. There would be no question of a continuing search and Geraldine would gain valuable days to withdraw the money and get to wherever it was she was going. I didn't lie. I simply let them believe what they wanted to believe. That's all I did.

Once the initial elation of my success had faded, a leaden weight slowly began to descend on my shoulders as I realized the many complications that this small act might now lead to. You see, if this wasn't Geraldine, then it was clearly some-body else, and it was only reasonable to assume that people would be looking for her. There might be friends. There might be anxious relatives. Since this was a murder, there was undoubtedly a murderer. I began to regret my subterfuge, but I could scarcely go back and say that I was no longer sure about the identification of the body and that I wanted a second look. At times I hoped that the police would of their own accord revisit the identity of the victim. But once I knew that the body must be Mary's – and that there were no grieving friends or relatives – I decided that perhaps I could leave things as they were a little longer.

So why was my deception never uncovered? Simple. When Mary Jones's body was found, nobody was looking for Mary Jones, only for Geraldine Tressider. The location and description were almost perfect. Why then should anyone want to doubt my identification? Later, when Mary Jones was finally reported missing, the police were looking for a lady with long mousy-coloured hair in the Bournemouth area. Why should they look again at the identification of a blonde lady found near Worthing and already confirmed as Geraldine Tressider? Of course, dental records would have shown them that they were wrong, but Geraldine's phobia about dentists meant that there were no dental records available for G. Tressider. Fingerprints and even DNA (I have no doubt) would have also indicated that something was amiss, but Geraldine had no fingerprints on record and I doubt that DNA tests would have been contemplated for a body that could be identified so quickly and easily. Still, it will not surprise you that I wanted to have that body cremated as soon as possible.

But knowing precisely where Mary Jones was did not help me know where Geraldine had vanished to. The days passed and I heard nothing. No messages on my phone – no messages on Geraldine's phone (which I kept going, just in case). You helped me discover that the money had been removed from the Swiss bank, so I knew that Geraldine had made it safely to Switzerland at least – but where then?

You were also quite right in believing that I was neither searching for Geraldine's killer (she wasn't dead) nor for the money (that was with Geraldine), but you couldn't work out what I was after. What I wanted to know was where Geraldine had gone and with whom. My growing fears were heightened by jealousy. I gave a number of people a tough time, I am sorry to say, as a result. That is why I did revel for a while in Smith's discomfort. Your well-timed (though wholly inaccurate) suggestion that they had actually been lovers did not help his cause in this respect one little bit. Young Darren Oxtoby was an unexpected possibility. So certain was I that he must know something that I actually demanded openly to know where Geraldine was. When his bafflement at my question confirmed that he was as ignorant as I was, I quickly covered up by pretending that I had been referring to Charlotte. My questioning of Dennis was equally direct, though you and he must have thought that I was crazy. Yet he *was* a possible accomplice and I had to take some risks to be certain that he was not involved. Rupert was the only one I was certain of and whom I consistently felt sorry for.

No, that's not true. I also felt extremely sorry for me. As the leads gave out and no call came through I found myself with nothing to do except potter around and tie up the loose ends. I dealt with the estate, such as it was, and told the creditors to expect the worst. The photograph albums and other items that Geraldine had marked with her yellow dots (well done for spotting them, by the way) were boxed up for safe-keeping. You have them now yourself, apart from one or two large non-perishable items that are still at my flat.

It was not until December that Geraldine finally contacted me: a postcard from Bradford, as it happened. I was to catch a particular plane on a particular date in January. No other instruction. No promise that she would be there. Just that.

Just that.

I hope I am not boring you, Elsie? You are very quiet. Just drowsy? I'd open a window, but the rain is so heavy at the moment.

Not much more to tell though: just Geraldine's story, and I don't really know much more than you do. I can't tell you why she decided to leave Rupert. I can't tell you how she got the money out of Smith, except that I am quite, quite certain, that she didn't sleep with him. I can't tell you where she is. All I do know is that she is out there somewhere, and that I should be meeting up with her soon, if this isn't just another red herring. Good old Geraldine, the queen of herring sellers, compared to whom I am a mere apprentice.

I don't expect you to approve. Fairfax has certainly made his views clear. You see, I've committed a crime – several, in all likelihood. Of course, I can argue that, technically, I didn't mislead the police: they chose to mislead themselves. I can also argue, from a practical point of view, that what I did was harmless. Peters is dead and one bit of evidence more or less makes no difference now to the case. But I didn't know that at the time. I have withheld a vital piece of evidence from the police. What if Peters had killed again? I have also knowingly aided and abetted Geraldine in goodness knows how many frauds. These are not things that Fairfax is likely to overlook or forgive. I'll never write another Fairfax story.

But you at least should know not to judge me by Fairfax's standards, though I have to point out that here was your *other* mistake. You thought that this was a detective story. In fact, it was a love story all along. What I did, I did for her. The rules are different for love stories. Romeo can kill Tybalt and still be a good guy. At least I've never knowingly stabbed anyone's cousin in a drunken brawl.

Asleep yet? Almost? Yes, Elsie, that's right: I did put something in the hot chocolate. Not poison, obviously – I want somebody to drive the car back to Findon. One thing we crime writers know about is what constitutes a lethal dose. So it's just enough to put you out for a few hours. After all, I don't want you following me to the check-in to see where I am going, do I? Once I knew that you were onto me I also knew that I had to be absolutely sure where you were when I was catching the plane. You'll be safe enough in the car until you wake up – in time for a good breakfast, hopefully. They do chocolate croissants at the airport cafeteria, I believe. I'll leave you the spare set of car keys and the money for the car park. There's enough petrol in the tank to get you home. And by that time, I'll be . . . where, I wonder?

Don't try to fight it. What I've given you is harmless but pretty strong. We're almost onto the motorway now. And look, do you see that? The rain's almost stopped now. There are stars up there, Elsie. Plenty of clouds, but here and there a bright star.

Of course, I don't know what I'm going to find when I get to Gatwick. Geraldine in person? Another instruction? Then another? Or will I find nothing at all?

I don't know, and for the moment I don't care. All I know is that I feel marvellously alive, as I haven't for years. Whatever I find at the check-in desk, nothing can take away from me the thrill that I have felt since I got that card from Geraldine. Perhaps she'll be there. Perhaps I'll have to pursue her halfway round the world.

But whichever it is, Elsie, I've made up my mind. I've always wanted one. Plenty of other people seem to have them and I really don't see why I shouldn't have one too. I'm going to get a life, Elsie. It's a happy ending.

I'm going to get a life.

Twenty-nine

Or, then again, not.

That's the problem with two narrators. (Crap idea, as I may have observed before.) Two narratives, two truths, two endings.

Of course Ethelred may have said all that stuff to me as he drove to his doom, but how would I know? I remember getting into his car and feeling a bit woozy. Then there was this dream about penguins. My next clear recollection is waking up in the short-stay car park with a couple of kids outside yelling, 'The dead witch moved! The dead witch moved!' I rolled down the passenger window and taught them a few witch-words, which would result in a slap round the face if they repeated them within striking distance of a responsible parent or guardian. Then I worked out how to extract myself from the car and went off and had a healthy chocolate-rich breakfast.

I was aware from the moment I got into the terminal that all was not quite as it should be – with hindsight it was a sort of shocked hush, but at the time it didn't mean much and I was looking for a coffee shop rather than a television screen. It was only as I was on my way back to the car park that I stopped to catch the latest news and just caught a blurred image of a plane tumbling from the sky in a mess of smoke. 'Amateur photograph,' it read, which didn't give much of a clue as to who was on it. Even then I worked out the percentage chances of it being Ethelred (low) and passed on with a shrug. It was only when they published a passenger list that I was certain – but that was days later.

I drove back to Sussex listening to the radio. The early reports were of an engine failure on a plane taking off from Gatwick. The later reports said it was a bomb. Then some smug bastard popped up to say that we should not jump to conclusions, but he could have saved his breath because we all had. I listened for a bit, then switched it off. Back at Ethelred's I did a quick search for clues, choco-late etc. and found his latest work, which (with a few amendments and improvements by yours truly) you have just read. The final chap-ter had clearly been written in advance of his actual journey to the airport, while he waited for me to drive down from London. Good old Ethelred – a writer to the very end.

In a strange way modern life caught up with Ethelred only with his death. He scarcely belonged to the twentieth century, let alone the twenty-first. Take his books – the historical ones were historical (obviously) but even the Fairfax ones contained nothing that Agatha Christie could not have written. His criminals were white working-class villains or toffs who had gone to the bad. Nobody used a mobile. Nobody seemed to have heard of the Internet. He wore clothes his father might have discarded in the fifties. He holidayed at old-fashioned hotels in the Loire. Ironic then that he should have died in such an up-to-the-minute way – blown up by a terrorist's bomb in mid-air. They never found his body, of course.

What more is there to say?

Not much, but there is still one thing that I need to explain –

there never was a chance of the poor sod having a happy ending. I think Ethelred had some sort of fixation about his Penkwen and Hedhog story. He saw himself as the Penkwen and Geraldine as the Hedhog to whom he would eventually be reconciled – 'in a faraway land', as he wrote. But that was never going to happen. If he had caught up with her, she would just have led him the same dance that she did before. Do you watch those wildlife programmes, where penguins get dragged off the ice floe and devoured by killer whales? No tender reconciliations there, I think you'll find. If there's one thing Geraldine isn't, it's a round cuddly Hedhog. If Ethelred wanted the genuine article he should have looked closer to home.

Sorry – I don't know quite why I said that. It's not as though I fancied Ethelred or anything. And vice versa, I assume. And love's all bollocks, as we have cordially agreed on several occasions in the past. But he needed looking after and I could have done that. Couldn't I? I could have followed him to his faraway land and been his Hedhog. Too late for that now.

And then again . . . I can't quite get it out of my mind . . . what if he wasn't on the plane? It's possible, isn't it? What if, to throw me off the scent, he booked two flights. The final red herring. What if he'd checked in for that flight, hand luggage only, then slipped away clutching a clever little false passport and caught another one entirely? And the first airline never amended their passenger list? Because they never found a body and (as all good crime writers know) until you've found the body, anything might have happened. So maybe there's a third ending to the story.

Maybe one day an unsigned card will turn up from Belize or Brisbane with instructions on how to adjust the central-heating system for the winter. Or maybe I'll be checking his mail and I'll see that somebody has used his credit card in Bogotá or Bombay. And I'll get straight on a plane and check it out.

Of course, that will never happen. But in the meantime, for some reason I can't quite pin down, I sit here, and I watch, and I wait.

In the Beginning

And one day the penkwen and the hedhog met again in a far-away land

Olrite sed the penkwen I am sory I sed you were too small and spiky

Olrite sed the hedhog I am sory I sed you were too big and flappy I would like to be your friend all wace Will you all wace be my friend?

They sed I should not trust you sed the penkwen

No, you can trust me sed the hedhog

Truly sed the penkwen?

Yes sed the hedhog and the hedhog smiled

Then I will be your friend sed the penkwen All wace

And that is all I know abut the hedhog and the penkwen

So that is the end of my story

Acknowledgements

I am grateful to all those who have given me help during the production of *The Herring Seller's Apprentice*. In particular I would like to thank Will and the team at MNW for their advice and support. I should also like to thank my son Tom, who (many years ago) produced the original and best version of 'The Penkwen and the Hedhog'.